When the Butterfly Falls

When the Butterfly Falls

Kamryn Adams

IMPRESA BOOKS

Published by Impresa Books

Impresa Books
The Kamryn Adams Group, LLC

10 9 8 7 6 5 4 3 2 1

Publishers Note
This is a work of fiction. All events and characters in this story are solely the product of the author's imagination. Any similarities between any characters and situations presented in this book to any individuals, living or dead, or actual places and situation are purely coincidental.

ISBN 978-0-990871316 (Paperback)
Printed in the United States of America

For everyone who has ever heard me say,
"I love you."

AUTHORS NOTE

This is a work of fiction. All events and characters in this story
are solely a product of the author's imagination; any
similarities between any characters and situations presented in
this book to any individuals living or dead are purely
coincidental and not intended by the author.

PROLOGUE

Growing up under the cast iron opinion and leather belts of my Aunt Janice, I was warned about two kinds of men: typical and tropical. I was told that "typical niggas" came from places like Detroit, Memphis, Atlanta, DC, Philadelphia, and Duluth. "Tropical niggas" came from an island somewhere.

Aunt Janice had a particular hatred for boys from uptown New York City...Harlem. She and my mother grew up in a brownstone just off of Lenox Avenue on 118th street and she had a firm belief that "no good man comes from Harlem". Since technically Manhattan is an island I could never quite figure out if Harlem boys were considered typical or tropical. Maybe that's why my Aunt Janice hated them so much, because they represented both. In either case, Aunt Janice did not have to worry about the boys and me.

Back to my earliest memories I cannot recall having a genuine love for anyone. Never mind a boy. I did not have sisters, brothers or "play cousins" to give me a fondness for other human beings. I certainly did not care much for Aunt Janice or any of the "uncles" that she dated along the way. Love was not something I found to be a real emotion.

By our adolescent years all the girls, except me, had taken an interest in boys. I paid no attention to them at all and it was not only because Aunt Janice had put the fear of God in me about getting pregnant like my "fast ass" mother had done. I just did not understand how the mere presence of a boy made girls act so stupid. More importantly, I never understood how a boy could be the cause of a girl fight and feuding that lasted half our young lifetime.

Looking back, I do not think I ever developed a true appreciation for the opposite sex. Don't misunderstand me. I'm not gay. I just never found anyone of the opposite sex to turn me on...to excite me. I never got sweaty palms or butterflies in my stomach for anyone, not even Michael Jackson in that yellow sweater or Prince in Purple Rain.

I never flopped across the bed and listened to love songs while dreaming of a boy who would sweep me away from Aunt Janice and all my misery. I did not wish for my first kiss and refused to talk about what it would be like when a boy finally "felt me up".

There was no tragic incident in my past with a boy or man that turned me off of them. I was not molested by my uncle or beaten by my father. The truth was that I didn't dislike boys. I was simply and completely unmoved by the presence of their dirty fingernails and crude humor.

But by the time I was fourteen I had learned to fake it in order to sit at the "cool table" in the cafeteria and get invitations to the best parties. Boy crazy equaled popularity in middle school and high school, which led into being a sorority girl in college. Though often entertained I was still not moved by men beyond a contrived giggle.

I had learned over the years what kinds of things women were supposed to like and dislike about men. In fact, I had gotten very good at mimicking delight and/or anger over male behavior. Sometimes I convinced myself that I was actually experiencing something inside only to find it was an emotional mirage.

Despite the inability to feel anything positive (or even negative) for a man, I was never in short supply of male companionship. Perhaps that is because a man's nature is to hunt for a challenge. I was never that interested in them so they were all the more interested in me.

It is the human paradox of relationships. We want what appears not to want us more than we want what actually loves us. The eighty-twenty rule, blah blah blah. There are many more ways to describe the fickle nature of humans in relationships and I had made myself a valuable commodity by exploiting them all to build the wonderful career as a skilled psychiatrist.

Then Kane Taylor walked into my office. That's when life changed for me. Well, not exactly at the precise moment. There was no "love at first sight". I do not believe in such things. As a psychiatrist, I try to get my patients to realize the flaw in such Hollywood drama. Love is built upon an intimacy that can only be developed over time. "At first sight" could be an intense attraction, but love it is not.

Kane had been coming to my office for months. The first time I saw him I felt the same way I did when I laid eyes upon the other 10 million men in the metro area...nothing. Men approached me hundreds of times in a week and getting a man's attention had become quite unconscious for me like breathing or blinking. So having Kane Taylor sweat me had just become a part of my day like going to the bathroom or having my morning coffee.

Each time Kane sauntered up the hallway the Versace cologne hit me before he walked through the door. I wondered why a package delivery guy would choose to wear Versace cologne. I assumed it was a gift from a woman. Whenever a man has an out of place element with him it is most always a gift from a woman. A new designer wallet from carrying no wallet at all, straight leg jeans from saggy graphic print denim, or a leather jacket on a guy who wears a wool overcoat screams that "a woman bought me this."

I cannot lie and say I never noticed how handsome he was. His smooth brown skin and clean shaven baby face were greatly appreciated by me. But, I gave him no regard. So it was not a surprise that Kane pursued me like a wolf. I ignored him and so he wanted to win. He needed to win. They all do.

Kane was cute in that unpolished "fake it til you make it" kind of way. I could not see the value in having sex with him just yet. He didn't appear to have money, status, or a particular skill I needed - like bringing my furniture to the second floor when I had not purchased white glove delivery service.

Besides, sex at that time had yet to produce an orgasm in my nearly twenty years of doing it. It had produced cars, jewelry, and a big house in the burbs - so sex was an undisputed necessity. But that whole make-my-legs-shake thing had never happened to me. However, I ought to have a gold statue on the mantle for my delivery of the big "O". Like when Harry met Sally and Billy Bob screwed Halle, I gave an Oscar worthy performance in the bed every time. My acting skills coupled with a gargantuan alpha male ego made for big fun in the sack.

One day I smelled Versace cologne pouring through my doorway. I am not sure why that particular day was the day, but it was the smell of "the game" that made me stand up behind my desk ready to play a little. This guy had been on me for months so I figured, "What the hell!"

I had pretty much given up on any man getting me to orgasm but maybe this delivery guy could give me a good workout like some of the other handy men in my past. My girls knew I hated to exercise. I would rather eat little, sleep much, and exercise my booty, not my body. That's what sex had become to me... cardio.

As Kane entered my office I sat on top of my desk with my legs crossed and I folded my arms across my chest. The look of surprise on his face was priceless. I was glad to have worn my skinny red pumps. I made sure that one of them hung off the back of my heel. Guys find that sexy. It's like the undressing part has already begun.

"Hey there," I smiled. "Let's do something different today. Let's have you deliver packages without asking me out and let me accept the packages without having to reject you again."

I leaned back and rested my elbows on the desk. I made sure to wiggle my pelvis a little to see if he diverted his eyes. He did.

"Hmmm, or how about I just turn around and take this package from the Apple store out to my truck and open it myself. I can download the new 2K12 and spend the rest of the day playing with the gift you bought for me." He strolled across my office and wiggled the package though the air.

"My new iPad!" I squealed in the way girls act when they get things they want. Though my feelings for men were counterfeit, my feelings for electronic gadgets were as genuine as Marc Kaufman fur.

"Say, 'I want it'. Then I might give it to you."

He had the nerve to lick his lips after that remark. The grin that stretched across his face was sinister but cute all at the same time. Not sure how you pull that off, but he did it.

I forced myself not to smile at his clever rhetoric. But, the more he walked in my direction taunting me with my package, my eyes lit up and a big smile instinctively spread across my face. Men don't excite me, but "the game"... now that gets my blood pumping.

"Yes I'd like my package. I will gladly sign for it," I said and tossed my hair over my shoulder. Men are visual and those kinds of things get their minds working overtime.

Kane held out his electronic clipboard. I scribbled a squiggle. With my eyes scanning the fine brown package standing in front of me, I tried to grab the box from Kane's hands. He would not let go of it. I grabbed at it again. He still held on to it. Finally I looked up directly into his eyes. They were light brown with specks of gold, which was unique for someone of his complexion. Before that day, I had never noticed them.

"Thank you," he said and let go of the package. "You know Dr. Goodwyn, there are other ways to manage your sexual attraction to someone besides avoidance." He took his hand and cupped my chin. His soft touch was a mismatch to his rough blue-collar hands. Again, must have been taught by a woman.

I made certain to stay firmly locked onto his face and I tried not to swallow. I realized that I was holding my breath so I let a small stream of air escape from my nostrils without making a sigh. My face got hot and I started to think I was embarrassed. I had never really been embarrassed before but I was sure that this was it. I glanced over at the mirror on the wall and my face was flush. I was blushing...for real. This guy made me blush. There was a feeling in my stomach that was like the drop from a roller coaster.

It was scary but exhilarating. I felt a little faint from holding my breath so I finally sighed. I had been in the presence of hundreds of men who touched my chin and licked their lips. There was something about Kane that just evoked "stuff" inside of me that I had never felt – for no reason at all.

"I enjoy human psychology and I've read that you should confront your unspoken desires head on," he said and then bit his bottom lip.

He moved in with a smile so genuine and adorable that it was hard not to smile back at him. He looked down at me and our foreheads were almost touching. I finally swallowed hard. "You read, huh?" My words came out in a whisper. I could not believe that I was actually being rendered a bit speechless. My throat had a lump that needed to be cleared so I made that quick, ugly gurgling sound which helped me gather my composure. My mouth was dry and I was pretty sure my panties were wet.

"Well now, Mr. Taylor," I said more forcefully. "The sign outside says Dr. Goodwyn doesn't it? So I am up on the desires of the human psyche, my friend. My desire for you is unspoken, because it's unborn. So the question is – do you think you can fill me with desire?"

I don't know what had come over me but I was not about to let this guy undo nearly twenty years of female ferocity. Up to this point in my life, I had remained in control of my emotions at all times. There had never been a man that could knock me off my game. Ever.

He laughed a sort of uncomfortable laugh. "Oh I think it's there already, but I can fill you up if you're asking for it. Your wish is my command." He leaned forward with a bow. It gave me just a second to think.

"Well, my friend. In the words of the ghetto boys, your mind is playing tricks on you." I shrugged and moved out of his shadow that loomed over me.

"Ghetto boys?" He roared with masculine laughter. "Oh that's hot. Okay, I see you Doc. Hip Hop fan are you?" He stepped back and put his hand over his mouth like he was sizing me up for a new dress. "I'll admit I'm surprised. I didn't see that in you. Hip Hop, huh?"

Once I saw that I had won this battle I figured I better back out gracefully before he got heated up again. I'd save my fun with Mr. Taylor for another day. But soon, I'd have to get with him again. He definitely intrigued me.

"Well, Mr. Taylor. Thank you for delivering my new iPad. I'm very excited."

"Yeah, so, uh, you are one of those technology freaks, huh?" He scrunched up his nose like he smelled hot garbage. Then pulled out a Motorola flip phone.

"Seriously? Wow!" I shook my head. "Actually you look like a technology dinosaur carrying that phone from the turn of the century."

"They did not have cell phones in 1900 so don't exaggerate." He said proudly.

I tilted my head and frowned, "Okay, but they did have them in 2000."

"Okaaaay..?" he said. "What's your point?"

"...which was the turn of THIS century. No?" My hands landed on my hips awaiting a reply.

He thought for minute and chuckled. "Okay, you got me on that." We both laughed. "I need my phone to talk to people. That's all. Not to watch videos, play games, or take pictures of big chicks in small clothes."

I burst into laughter. "I can admit that I do like my gadgets if you can admit that your phone is an antique."

He twisted his lips - very nicely. "Are you are one of those pretty babes that sits in Starbucks displaying sexy pics on The Facebook to everyone looking over your shoulder?"

"Not exactly. I'm not technically on 'the Facebook' as you say, other than advertising for my practice. But I do love Starbucks. I'm a gold card member. " I reached behind me and pulled my card from the basket on my desk. "See." As soon as I said it I wanted to take it back. Starbucks gold card props? Really Farah? My behavior had turned down right foolish like the school girls I used to secretly despise.

"So, why don't I meet you at Starbucks sometime," Kane suggested.

"Do you know I'm married?" I asked and flashed my diamond-encrusted band.

"Do YOU know you're married, Dr. Goodwyn," he said with twisted lips. "If I had a wife, I hope she would not sit on the desk with her sexy legs dangling for the delivery guy."

"Very funny. Yes, I know I'm married. Which is why I cannot go out on a date with you."

I almost laughed aloud. It sounded completely ridiculous coming from my freely active lips. The truth was that I had never stopped dating since the day I met my husband. If my girls had been there, they would have been rolling on the floor laughing at me. Hysterically. I did try for six-months after our wedding because I thought I might be able to actually bond with a man. That ended when I ran into one of the hosts on the sports network news. The girls and I scored a completely sponsored trip to the Pro Bowl behind that one.

Despite what I considered a most pitiful attempt to sound like a faithful and doting wife, Kane bought it. "What if I just happened to show up at Starbucks when you are there? Then it's not a date and you are technically not having coffee with me. We will be just having coffee in the same place." He raised his eyebrows and waited for an answer.

All kinds of declining statements ran through my head. I did not like the way this guy was making stuff happen to my body on the inside. I needed to stay far away from him.

But when I opened my mouth all that came out was "Whatever. It's a free country."

Oh my goodness! I sounded like a sixth-grader. I was a chocolate MYLF that had seduced my share of actors, rappers, meter readers, and male nurses. How was the delivery guy making me flush on the inside?

"Bet," he said and turned around in his Timberland boots and brown work pants. "I'll see you there Wednesday between eight and eight-fifteen. He walked out with a swag I had never seen on him before that day.

He threw out a time and I did not disagree so I guess it was set. It's not a big deal. Besides, it's just coffee.

-1-

When Farah arrived at Starbucks on Wednesday, she sat down at a table near the front window and opened her iPad. Kane had been waiting for her in the back near the restroom. He strolled across the room singing "There goes my baby" by Usher. Farah was all smiles. When he sat down at a table directly across from her she looked surprised as if she had forgotten their scheduled "accidental" meeting until that moment.

"We are not here together," he said. Her eyes told him that she was delighted with their decision NOT to have coffee together. Farah grinned and moved her bag from the empty chair at her table but Kane stayed seated at his table.

Farah had spent quite a bit of time thinking about Kane over the last few days. You can sit with me," she said and motioned for him to approach her.

"Nope, you never agreed to have coffee with me," he said. "You are a married woman and I respect that."

Farah was glad someone respected her marriage, even if she did not. They carried on a two-table conversation for nearly three hours. That's when Farah learned that there was a lot more to this delivery guy than Versace cologne and great smile.

To her surprise, Kane was a rather intelligent and well-informed man. He had a lot of different interests - everything from dominos to deep sea diving. Farah found out that Kane had gone to college on a football scholarship, but lost his scholarship eligibility when he sold some autographed memorabilia, which is a violation of NCAA rules. At that point he had to return to Harlem and find a "good job".

She could tell that his lack of a degree made him a little insecure because he was such a vocal critic of what he called "college-educated idiots that lacked common sense." He validated his position for over twenty minutes as he shared the growing list of rich and famous people who had dropped out of college, which was mostly a list of athletes, musicians, and actors.

Farah knew that Kane was hardly sold on his own position because he went on to talk about his aspirations to go back to school to become a psychologist. "I could never go to medical school to be a full blown shrink like you. I hate the sight of blood."

In the middle of mesmerizing Farah with his reading list of psychological textbooks, many of which she had read, Kane's phone buzzed. When he looked at it, Farah noticed that his eye twitched. The person called right back again. And again. And again.

"Maybe you should get it," Farah said. "Is it your baby mama?" she joked.

He frowned, "I don't have any kids. Do you?" Kane's face had an expectant expression.

"I have one daughter."

"What's her name?" Kane asked.

"None of your business," Farah frowned. "Not sure my daughter's name has anything to do with your plans for me."

Kane chuckled. "You never know."

Farah gasped with a laugh. "Ewww, you're one of those."

Kane's phone kept buzzing and he tried his best to ignore it. "It's probably my cousin," he growled.

"Probably? You don't have the number programmed into that high tech flip phone of yours?" Farah giggled. "It could be an emergency, so why don't you get it. I'll be right here." She winked.

Kane sneered, "Alright". He picked up the phone and as he walked away from Farah, "Hello! What do you want?"

"What you are doing?" his cousin asked.

"You called me twelve times in a row. Damn! I'm having coffee," he said.

"Oh, uh-hu, and are you having coffee with the rich lady doctor?" his cousin taunted.

"Yes!" Kane snarled between clenched teeth.

"Excellent! Good work, cousin."

"I've got to go. Bye!" He slammed the phone closed.

He walked back to the table with a dumbfounded look on his face. He began to stutter. "I was right. That was my annoying cousin."

"I see. I could see you yelling in the phone at him." Farah said. "Is everything okay?"

"Yeah," Kane said. "Just needs a favor and has no patience to wait for me to do it."

"Family," Farah nodded to show she understood even though she did not.

"So tell me about your family," Kane asked and scooted his chair closer to her table without being at her table. She laughed at the gesture.

"I don't have family. I mean. I'm married. Of course you know that. I have my daughter. That's all I really have."

Kane looked concerned. "What about your parents? Siblings?"

"My mother died when I was very young. I don't remember her but I know she's there." Farah tapped her heart.

"What about your dad?"

"I don't know who my father is and neither did my mother, apparently." Farah smiled to ease the discomfort she saw on Kane's face.

"Wow! That's crazy. So who raised you? Grandparents?" he asked.

"My Aunt Janice, who would have hated you, by the way."

"Why?"

"Because you're from Harlem. So was she. Go figure."

He chuckled. "Yep. There are a quite few people who hate to return to Harlem. They escape to Jersey living and that's all. Smart people."

"I wouldn't call my aunt smart at all. I'd call her a bunch of other things though." Farah frowned at the thought of her Aunt Janice.

"Well, she clearly did something right. Look at you." He smiled at her and finally pulled his chair up to the table.

Farah felt warm inside as Kane pulled closer. There was no mistaking it. After all the years of faking those fuzzy feelings and butterflies, she actually had them now - for real.

"I am what I am despite being raised by her, not because I was raised by her. Trust me. It was not fun." She crossed her arms and leaned in toward the center of the table. "What about you? Tell me about your family."

"Okay, but don't try to analyze me, Doc."

"I promise," she said and playfully crossed her fingers in the air.

"That's what I thought," Kane said with a grin. "Well, my parents have been married for almost fifty years. I am a mama's boy. My father gets a little frustrated with me, but I know he loves me."

"Frustrated? Why?" Farah asked.

"Let's just say I've made some bad decisions along the way," Kane said.

"Do you have brothers and sisters?" Farah asked.

"Nope."

"An only child!" Farah squealed and the people at the next table looked over in alarm. "Okay, so I know you are spoiled, irresponsible, selfish, and arrogant."

Kane made a sour face, "Girl, aren't you an only child?"

"Yes, but I was raised by Aunt Janice. That did not afford me any form of self-indulgence or self-esteem. Never mind any entitlement or acceptance. Please!"

"Was it that bad?" Kane asked.

"It was that bad," she said, "and worse."

Kane found himself feeling sorry for Farah as she told him some of the stories of her childhood. She was beautiful, smart, successful and seemed like the world had been handed to her on a platinum platter. When, in fact, she had been through quite a bit before she even reached her teen years. Farah was nothing like Kane expected her to be. The antics she displayed in her office showed her as a bit of a vixen but now he saw that she had a very gentle place inside of her.

Kane looked in her eyes, "So your family, your husband and daughter, are really important to you, huh?"

"Very much so." Farah said. There was an awkward silence between them. "So I guess you are wondering why I am here with you then. Right? Why do I behave the way I do?"

"Well, kind of. Yeah," he said with half of a smile.

"Someone else would say 'I don't know' but I am a psychiatrist... and a damn good one. I am here with you because I have never really connected to my husband. I've never connected to any man for that matter. Honestly, my daughter was the first person in the world to evoke feeling in me that I can recall. I was overcome with emotion the first time I held her in my arms." Farah looked off as if looking back in time. "I mean... it was like nothing I could explain. I felt like a warm blanket was tossed over my head and suffocating me with dedication, kindness, patience, honesty, and sacrifice. It was love."

"Wow" Kane's eyes misted over and he looked away from Farah.

Farah could see pain in Kane's eyes. She recognized it since she saw it every day, patient after patient. She changed the tone of the discussion to ease whatever was going on in

Kane's mind at that moment.

She continued, "It's actually very common for people

who grow up without both of their parents to be missing a link

with humanity. Not that there is something physically wrong

with their ability to love. The hearts and minds of these

people work like everyone else's in the beginning. But, they

often subconsciously kill that emotion and refuse to

acknowledge that there is some type of invisible connection

between humans that makes them care for each other. If we

embrace the notion that we are a bunch of individuals with no

spiritual interconnection, then we don't hurt as much being

separated from our parents."

"We?" Kane asked.

"Yes, I am one of these people. I shut my emotions

down a long time ago - so long ago I can't remember. In a

way, I'm worse than other people because I completely

understand what the problem is but I still cannot correct it. For

most people it is subconscious. But for me, I am well aware of

my issues."

"So how does that work? I mean, what does it feel like?"

"Honestly, unless I'm with my daughter, I feel like a flesh covered robot."

"That's deep."

"Yeah, it is." Farah said with a smile.

"So you think not knowing your dad is why you don't like men?"

Farah laughed. "Who said I don't like men? I really enjoy men. That's actually the problem. That's why I'm here with you," she paused. "Anyway...back to you. So you don't have siblings but you have cousins."

"How did you know that?" Kane asked with raised eyebrows.

"Umm because you said it was your cousin on the phone."

"Oh...yeah," Kane rolled his eyes. "My mother had two brothers..."

"Had?"

"Yeah, they died together in a car crash."

"That's how my mother died." Farah's tone was matter of fact. "That's awful."

"It's awful that they died, but not that they died together. They did everything together. It was wild. They were best friends. They worked together. They even got married together. They married sisters."

"Get out of here! Your uncles were married to sisters?"

"Yep, my cousins are double-kin, as they say down south."

"That's cool," Farah said.

"Did I mention my uncles were twins? My cousins look a lot alike. Some people think they are twins, but they are completely different. One is focused and responsible. The other is wild and destructive."

"The one on the phone?" Farah asked.

"Yes," he said. "Always trying to pull me into drama and schemes." Kane looked off into the distance again.

"And why do you allow him to do that to you?" Farah went into work mode. "Do you feel like you own him something? If you know he is wild and destructive, why not separate your self from him?"

"That's a good point." Kane nodded and fell off into thought. "But I always felt bad. I can still remember the faces from my uncles' funeral. I was young but I remember how devastated everyone was. Especially my cousins."

"Well, give him my card. Maybe I can help make a connection between the grief and the 'wild and destructive' behavior."

"Uh, thanks but my cousin would never agree to that." Kane reflected for a moment. "Anyway, enough about my family. I want to hear more about you. What's your favorite color?" Kane asked.

"Black."

"Whose favorite color is black?" he laughed.

"Mine," Farah asserted. "Black is sexy and demure."

"True." Kane nodded. "What's your favorite food?"

Farah stopped him. "Do we really have to do the whole "favorite" thing like a first date?"

"Naw, I guess not." Kane looked at his watch.

"I'm glad we didn't have coffee together today." Farah smiled. She began to wrap up the conversation because she knew Kane had packages to deliver. "I enjoyed our talk. You turned out to be a lot different than I anticipated. There is much more to you than meets the eye, Mr. Taylor."

He took his hand and swiped a strand of hair behind her ear. "Likewise. And thanks for the mini-session. It helped me put things into perspective."

"How so?" she asked.

"It just did." Kane said.

"So, will I see you again? For a real date maybe?" Farah asked.

"Is that what you want, Farah? To jeopardize your family by going out with me?"

"If not you, it would be someone else. Trust me." She sighed. "It's who I am."

"Don't beat yourself up. You've been through a lot. I get why you became a psychiatrist."

"Kane, stop making me sound like little orphan Annie. I am a grown woman. I am well in control of my behavior.

Besides, I told you my daughter was the first person that ever made me feel anything."

"Yeah…so."

"And so…you are the second." Farah looked at him and Kane could see in her eyes that she was telling the truth. She looked away quickly. When she looked back toward him she was welled with tears. "It's true. The other day in the office I was so…so embarrassed."

"Embarrassed?" Kane roared in laughter. "That's not what I was going for, but I'll take it."

Farah giggled, "I know. I know. But hey, that's a big deal for me. I felt something."

Suddenly she was overcome by her own emotion again. This was foreign for her and she was getting overwhelmed by this "stuff" that was going on inside of her.

"I spent years wishing I could be emotionally normal. Then I just gave up and decided to be me. After that I decided that if I couldn't help myself I could be an objective voice to help others in pain."

"Doc, 'normal' is highly overrated." Kane leaned over and kissed her on the cheek. "Dinner and movie this weekend?"

"Sure." Farah smiled and wiped the small tears that begun to fall from her eyes.

"Good. Maybe this time you can feel something besides embarrassment." He grabbed her chin in a playful manner. Then, he kissed her cheek and walked out the door.

She was definitely feeling something other than embarrassment. It was foreign. She had no idea why or how this man had penetrated her deadened emotions, but she was kind of certain that she liked it. In the hours that they had been talking, Farah did not spend a single moment thinking about sex with Kane. She didn't think about what he could offer her or how he might be able to make her life a little easier. She was genuinely interested in what he had to say and learning more about him. For the first time in her life, Farah was intrigued by a man.

"Mother," she looked down at her heart, "I think I'm in trouble."

-2-

By the time Farah got home from the hospital the house was dark and silent. She was thankful everyone had gone to sleep. She was grateful for any time she could daydream about Kane. It had been an amazing couple of weeks with him and the newness of "emotion" had begun to grow on her.

She slipped by Talcum, the bright white terrier they bought as a gift for Bryann's tenth birthday. There was a half-bottle of diet cola in the refrigerator so she filled her glass. It wasn't exactly what she wanted. She took two sips from the glass and carefully placed it into the sink still more than three-quarters full. What she really wanted was a glass of Shiraz.

Farah was well aware that alcohol was her foe but sometimes she just wanted a little taste of wine. Actually, it was a little more than sometimes and a little more than a taste. Though it took her four years to accept it and seek help, she knew during her first year of medical school that she was an alcoholic. Her professor taught on the genetic and psychological causes of addiction. Tragically losing her mother at such a young age, never knowing her father, and living under the God awful rule of her Aunt Janice made it almost inevitable that Farah would end up with some sort of a serious vice. All in all, she did not find alcohol to be such a bad one in context of crack, gambling, and self-mutilation.

Farah went upstairs, slipped into her grey satin nightgown and curled up in the bed next to her husband, Greg. He snored like something from the Bronx Zoo. Even with the obnoxious sounds blowing from his nose and mouth, he looked gorgeous stretched out in his side of the bed.

From the moment she met him on campus, Farah knew that he was the kind of guy Aunt Janice wanted her to marry. Twenty years later, he was still one of the finest men she had ever laid eyes upon. He was smart, handsome, and came from a good family.

Back then, he reminded her of Chachi from Happy Days. At forty-one, he still had an amazing body because he constantly refused carbohydrates and consumed a bolus of protein every few hours. With just a few sprouting grays, Greg was still topped with a full head of shiny, dark hair and people regularly stopped to tell him that he looked like Scott Baio. Farah had the hottest and richest husband in the neighborhood. Despite all the hotness that she could attest to, she had no desire to have sex with him.

After all the years of marriage she was over it. Sex had gotten boring and predictable with Greg. It was one thing not to have an orgasm but to be bored on the way to an uneventful finish was just unacceptable to Farah. She could not muster the devotion to put herself through it.

Back in college, Farah and Greg had sex incessantly. Farah's motivation was to take Greg off the market. Greg's motivation was to let the entire dorm know how well he pleased a woman. She kept riding him like Sea Biscuit until one day they landed in the current state - married.

Farah felt like nobody could judge her for that because all women do it. Women rock your world as often as possible to get you over the hump - pardon the pun - then after marriage the amount of vaginal folly diminishes significantly. It is why sex cannot be the cornerstone of a relationship. Men do things to get sex. Women give sex to get things done.

Farah understood a man's needs so she hooked him up when she absolutely could not avoid it anymore. Sometimes she offered a sexy striptease while he pleasured himself. Other times, she had to simply endure it. In the past, Farah could not bring herself to make love to Greg without a half-glass of wine and a full dose of Valium. This explained why their sex life had gone down hill since her sobriety. In addition to the libido draining effects of her job, Greg's lack of enthusiasm for anything other than making money just turned her off completely. Direct deposit on payday was Greg's idea of an exciting time.

Right after they married Farah started medical school and he was finishing up his MBA at Wharton. Bryann came shortly after that. More and more time went by between sexual encounters and before they knew it, sex had taken a back seat to parenting, work, and must-see TV.

Though she tried not to wake him, Greg rolled over with a grunt and kissed Farah on the cheek. He got up out of bed and stumbled to the bathroom. His tight, bare butt moved across the floor, which was impressive to her eyes but did nothing between her thighs. It took her years to get used to the fact that Greg slept completely naked. He thought it was odd that she slept with anything on at all. In a debate over which was more common, Farah simply pointed out that there was a billion dollar pajama industry for a reason.

A few seconds later, there was a quick splash in the water before Farah heard Greg's urine splatter on the back of the seat and undoubtedly all over the floor. "Hit the water Mr. Goodwyn," she said before being answered by a flush of the toilet.

After she heard Greg wash his hands, Farah watched him walk across the floor slinging water. "Would it kill you to use a towel?" she asked.

"Have I ever dried my hands in the twenty years you've known me?"

"No, and I've never understood why it's so hard to dry your hands instead of flinging water all over the floor."

"Doc, the definition of insanity is what?" He laughed.

Farah sighed. "Doing or seeing the same things over and over and expecting a different result." She muttered.

Farah wanted to hold a "10" sign for Greg's V-shaped upper body and perfect thighs. She had a great appreciation for Greg's mind, his body, and his dedication to their family. She simply could not turn that appreciation into anything more than a deep respect and a brotherly kind of love. Greg was her friend and she loved him as such. She thought of Greg as someone she could hook up with one of her girlfriends. You know, the guy that you think is great and handsome but he just doesn't do it for you. That's who Greg was to Farah.

"And I am so tired of you splashing pee on the floor," she said.

"Well as much money as I make why don't you hire someone to clean it up? You are the only woman on the block without a housekeeper. Why you insist on cleaning the whole house is beyond me. In fact, I'm going to start calling you Maria."

"Greg!" she pushed him in the chest. "See, that's your racist mother in you."

"I'm just kidding," he said wrapped in an air kiss. "And my mother is not really racist. She just can't handle that I am married to such a smart and beautiful black woman like you."

"Which makes her a racist."

"Your Aunt Janice was a bit of racist too. How did she used to say it?" He threw up his hand and mimicked Aunt Janice's sing-song voice. "I can't stand a black man. He has no heart and he has no plan."

"Hmph! You said that with great conviction, Greg Goodwyn." Farah frowned with intensity to make sure he understood her disapproval.

"I was just joking. Since when are you psychoanalyzing my behavior around race? After 16 years of marriage, nonetheless."

"Since I started to notice how smug you get when we are together and a Black man approaches. You look at him like you are better than him and it's like you're taunting him because you have me. As I think about it, you even did that in college."

"What the hell are you talking about?" Greg raised his voice. "I don't think I am better than a man just because of the color of his skin. And yeah, I probably do look smug. Not because I am a white man but because I am a man. I'm a man who happens to be married to the most beautiful woman in the world and one of the smartest most brilliant psychiatrists in America. So yeah, I'm the lucky one. And yeah, I look at the other guy like he's a loser because compared to what I have on my arm he is. Race has nothing to do with it."

"Whatever Greg." Farah refused to be flattered.

"Don't 'whatever' me. What has gotten into you? Why all this racial stuff all the sudden? Have you forgotten my best friend is Black - the longest friend I've had in life?"

"Adam is a Bergen County, Yale-educated, seven-figure..." she stopped.

When they first got engaged, Greg made Farah promise never to use the N-word, even in jest. He hated that African-Americans had embraced the word despite its negative genesis. Keeping that promise was a chore for Farah having grown up around Aunt Janice's complete mastery of the word's use.

When Farah forgot something that her aunt had asked of her it was deemed "nigganesia". When Farah landed the lead role in the school play, her Aunt Janice exclaimed "nigganificent"! She heard variations of the word so much that it became like a separate language in their household.

Consequently, Farah's first day of kindergarten was quite memorable. When the teacher asked her to introduce herself to the class, five-year-old Farah shrugged and repeated verbatim what she had heard many times from her Aunt Janice, "I could be nigganese, niggarean, or just a pure-bred nigga. Who knows?"

Farah knew her husband was not a racist. She sometimes questioned whether he was truly white. He didn't sky dive, rock climb or any of those other thrill-seeking activities that white folks loved. He absolutely hated to be in the water and preferred to eat chicken, mashed potatoes, and green beans over anything else possible in the world of culinary creation. Greg had never seen an episode of "Friends" and turned down free tickets to the NHL Stanley Cup because it was "too cold in there".

In fact, Greg was completely risk-averse except when it came to his investments. Greg flipped money like he had people working corners in Brooklyn. His excitement around the monthly finance statements and his ability to turn three thousand dollars into ten thousand dollars had him beating his chest in the bedroom mirror. When that ten thousand dollars became fifty thousand he became a fan of his own genius.

Once Farah walked in on him and it was reminiscent of Al Pacino in Scarface. He was having a "the world is mine" moment. Greg was purely Anglo-Saxon but because of some of his behaviors Farah rarely ever thought about the fact that he was White. He was simply Greg, her husband and friend.

Greg loved the ground Farah walked on. He was smart, handsome, made loads of money and took great care of her. He footed the bill for her to open her private practice, paid off her medical school loans and gave Farah anything she wanted. He gave her a bunch of stuff she never even thought about having, like the museum-sized home where they currently lived. Greg looked so good on paper that Farah truly felt like she had no reason to complain about him other than her own feelings - or lack thereof.

"Sweetheart, how did me peeing on the floor get us to this?" he asked with a tender kiss to her forehead.

It made her think of the way Kane had drawn so close to her the other day in the office. She could not take her mind of him. The conversation at Starbucks was refreshing. So refreshing that she did not even think of having sex with him. Although she was hot for Kane, there was something else that Farah found interesting about him.

-3-

A few days later the phone rang as Farah was getting out of the shower. She could hear Greg speaking "uh-hu", "okay", and "I understand". His voice sounded tight so Farah walked out of the bathroom in her towel.

"What's up?"

Greg held up one finger. "Okay, Alan. Thank you. I'll get back to you once I discuss it with Farah." He hung up the telephone.

"Discuss what with me?" Farah flopped onto the bed next to Greg. His eyes were expressionless but he forced the corners of his mouth upward. He had that same look when he had to tell Farah that her grandfather had died. She braced herself for whatever was next.

"A letter from the South African agency," he said. Greg tried to keep his expression but Farah saw the grimace beneath the grin.

"What letter?"

Greg pulled his robe a bit tighter and explained. "Calm down. It's nothing bad," he said. "They sent a letter to Alan's office trying to reach us."

"Why are they writing to us?"

Greg sighed like he was preparing for Farah's response. "It seems that Bryann's birthmother has requested contact."

Farah's chest started to rise and fall rapidly. The tightness took her breath away. There was no way they could accommodate a meeting with Bryann's birth mother, who in Farah's mind was some guilt-stricken drug addict who now wanted a second chance at their daughter. She swallowed hard and began to cry. Hundreds of thoughts rushed through her head as quickly as her heart pounded. "What! Can she do that?"

"Alan is calling them back within the hour. Let's just see what they have to say before we panic. Calm down." Greg said.

Of course he wanted her to calm down. Greg had a horrible sense of urgency in Farah's opinion. Rather no urgency at all. It was a finance thing. Nothing really happened quickly in Greg's world. Everything in his world forecasted and either added up in the end or not. Greg said the best thing about being an accountant is that if the numbers fall short, you point a finger at sales. If costs run high you point a finger at operations. Bottom line, nothing was ever his fault. He was the messenger.

"Calm down?" Farah said. "What if she wants her back? What if they take her away from us? What if she doesn't like that you're white? Can they take her back for that? Can they do that? We have to tell Bryann right away, Greg. We have to do it now. "

"Farah, sweetie, slow down and breathe." Then, he replayed her words in his mind. He squinted and made a face like someone squirted lemon juice in his mouth. "What if she doesn't like me because I'm white?" His face scrunched even tighter. "Well, what if she's Afrikaner? People think Bryann is our child because she looks biracial. Her mother could be a white South African, like Charlize Theron or Harry Oppenheimer."

"Who the hell is Harry Oppenheimer?" Farah didn't know why she asked the question because she really did not give two damns about who the man was.

"A business man," Greg said with a smirk of pride spread through his smile.

She rolled her eyes, "Of course."

Deflated by her lack of enthusiasm for Oppenheimer, Greg shot another name at her. "Okay, Steve Nash. Does that appeal more to you?"

"Yes, but Steve Nash is Canadian," she said.

"He was born in South Africa." Greg boasted this knowledge. He had done such outstanding research before they adopted Bryann to make sure he knew everything about her homeland.

Before this little game of global jeopardy went on any further Farah came to her senses and screamed, "Greg, I don't care!" Her chest got even tighter and she thought she was having a heart attack. "Oh, a pain shot down my right arm. I'm going into cardiac arrest."

"Heart attacks shoot pain down your left arm, Dr. Goodwyn."

"Not with women. Many women have pain in their right arm, finance master. Either way… THIS IS GOING TO KILL ME!!!!

"Calm down. Gee! So dramatic." Greg smiled like he appreciated that side of Farah's personality.

"There is no way that I can lose my baby girl. Bryann has been with us since she was just days old. And every day since the day we brought her to the United States, I feared that her birth mother would want her back one day. It has been my greatest fear and a freaking Lifetime movie waiting to happen. We have to sit her down and talk to her."

Greg cleared his throat, which meant he was about to make a declaration as the M.O.T.H. -man of the house. His father does the same thing. "We agreed that we would never tell Bryann she was adopted. You can't go back on our agreement. I don't want her to know. She is our daughter. There is no reason to give her any other reality than that one."

"Greg, she's almost fifteen. She needs to know. There could be all kinds of implications for her. She's bipolar. For all we know her birthmother could be bipolar too."

He furrowed his brow in a way that Farah knew he wasn't going to budge. The MOTH had spoken and she retreated. "We are not going to burden Bryann with this. Period." Greg pointed at Farah. He meant business.

"Burden me with what?" In walked their skinny girl...without knocking again. As if she were four years old, she climbed into bed and snuggled in her parents bed among the pillows. "Are you guys arguing about me? I have been good, haven't I?"

"No," Greg said. "Unless you call hiding a naked boy and a bong under your bed 'being good'. And since when did they start making decorative bongs? You know you are too young to get high when your bong is purple with silver stars and butterflies. Geez!"

"Oh really," Farah leaned over and kissed her daughter's temple. She looked at Greg and asked, "And what would be the appropriate age to get high then, Dad?"

"You know what I mean," he said.

Bryann and Farah giggled.

"At no age should you get high ESPECIALLY with a...a..." he searched for the right words. "...Bedazzled bong."

"That was weeks ago, Daddy. C'mon." Bryann batted her eyes at him just like the first time he had ever seen her innocently swaddled in the hospital bassinet. "Plus I had missed my meds. Otherwise, I would never have done that and you know it."

Neither Greg nor Farah could deny that she was the most beautiful thing they had ever seen. Dark wavy hair, piercing grey eyes, and skin that was the color of creamer with a splash of coffee in it - she looked as if she were the product of Farah's cocoa brown skin and Greg's olive undertones.

"It should have never happened in the first place," Greg said sternly. "Stop making excuses for yourself."

Farah shot Greg a sharp look. He could have gone a little easier on her. Most of her antics were actually due to her illness and not necessarily that she was a bad child. Though, sometimes Bryann leveraged her illness to get away with things. As a mother and psychiatrist, Farah could always see through the facade.

"Daddy you are impossible to please." Bryann hopped out of the bed and stomped her skinny legs to the doorway. "I'm going to get dressed. Bye Mom." She tossed her head away from Greg to be sure he noticed she had ignored him.

"Bryann, I love you." Greg called out to her definitively. He locked the door and commenced to strip down to start getting dressed for the day. Farah stared at him with her lips pursed tight. "What?" he shrugged.

"Nothing." She rolled over with her back to him. Still lying there in her towel. She said a silent prayer to late her mother. "Mom, please help me."

Like many physicians, Farah was also challenged in her faith. If she acknowledged that there was an all-powerful God then she must also accept that the fate of the patient is not really in her hands. If that was the case, then why even become a physician?

Farah started talking to her mother when she was a little girl. She imagined that her mother was her guardian angel. As a child, she used to lie in bed and try to remember something about her mother. Anything. But she was not even a year old yet when she and her mother had the accident.

As she stared out across the room, Farah was haunted by thoughts of what things may come. She continued to face the wall. Without turning towards Greg - without a blink she asked, "What are we going to do?"

"Let's leave it to Alan. It's his job to handle this kind of thing for us."

"Yeah, but--"

"But what, Farah? Let's just wait and see what Alan says." Greg bent down and kissed Farah on the top of her head.

"You smell so good," she said.

"Oh do I?" Greg said and moved his hand under her towel.

She jerked away, "Greg please! I'm not interested in having sex when our daughter could be taken away from us."

"What a surprise! As if you are ever interested in having sex. Don't use this as an excuse." Greg's voice started to elevate before she shushed him.

Farah rolled over and turned her back to him once again. This time she pulled the covers up to her waist. While the guilt crept up into her chest she knew he was right. There was not an amorous bone in her body for him.

Greg walked across the room while he fixed his tie. He mumbled something under his breath. He stood in the middle of the room and stared at Farah lying there half naked under the bed sheet. "I don't want to argue with you about this, Farah. I am tired of arguing with you about this."

"But you know it's not my fault." Farah was disturbed by the whine that escaped from her lips. It was unattractive, even to her. "I have no libido."

Greg's face softened. He dropped his head and walked back toward the bed. "Sweetheart, I understand. I really do. But you don't even try. Why don't we try some of those creams and stuff?" Greg referred to the arsenal of sex toys and libido stimulating products that lay hidden in the bottom drawer of the nightstand – covered with dust.

Farah simply sighed. The truth was that Farah used sex to get things she needed in life. Greg gave her everything she needed so, in her mind, there was no reason to have sex with him. Her body could not respond to him. Oddly enough, it was because she cared for him that she couldn't get hot for him. In Farah's mind, sex was a way to destroy, manipulate, or capture a man. She had no need of any of that for Greg.

She definitely understood his need but wasn't up to the task - especially under these circumstances. Greg and Farah were partners, not lovers. They were partners who had worked together, played together, and built a life together. They were partners faced with a big problem at the moment. Losing Bryann - even sharing her with the birthmother - could be devastating for Farah. Bryann gave Farah the chance to

open her heart to someone in genuine love. Many mothers say
it in cliché but for Farah it was the very truth of her existence.
Bryann held the key to her heart. Bryann made her human.

-4-

On most days Farah enjoyed her five-minute commute to the office. But whenever there was something on her mind, she always wished she had a longer drive to sort it all out. Farah was consumed in thought. She knew that Bryann would hate her once she was told about the adoption. Worse than that, it would surely spin Bryann into an episode. The thought made Farah queasy in her stomach.

Greg and Farah were like most parents. When they made the decision to keep a secret from their daughter they disguised it in the desire to protect her. In reality it was usually selfish motives that caused parents to keep things from their children. All parents want their kids to think that they are perfect parents. Parents want their children to believe that they have all the answers. Most of all, parents want the children to always be their children.

In the case of closed adoption, many parents claimed it to be in the best interest of the child despite the agencies and psychologists who contend that an open adoption is best. Experts say that an open adoption, when there is some contact and awareness with the birth parent, produces better-adjusted children. Because this can challenge the traditional idea of "family", some parents choose to keep it a secret. Farah and Greg made that choice and it was now coming back to bite them. Actually, Greg made the choice and forced Farah to comply. It was the only way he would agree to an adoption.

The irony of adopting Bryann was not missed on Farah. Since Farah did not clearly understand her own genetic history, she refused to conceive children. She did not want her children to end up with the alcoholic gene or the depression that ultimately led to her mother's death. So, Farah convinced Greg to adopt a child. Their beautiful, perfect little baby girl was diagnosed with Bipolar Mania shortly before her eleventh birthday. Though ironic, Farah did not regret the adoption. In her view the bipolar disorder was not genetically her fault, so it was easier for Farah to deal with it without guilt, which was the most common emotion in her childhood.

When Farah pulled into the parking lot she sat for a minute to get her thoughts together. The moment had passed for her to focus on her own difficulties. It was now time for Farah to help her patients resolve their issues and medically correct their chemical imbalances.

Showing empathy to complete strangers was a gift because Farah was able to focus on the issue and not the person. She taught her patients to logically think through their problems as if it were happening to someone else. She helped them understand that mental disorders are no different than cardiovascular or respiratory disorders. They need to be treated with medication and it is more than okay to do so.

It was difficult for some people to accept medication, particularly people of color. Farah went through the same explanation with all of her patients. "You take your blood pressure medication to treat your high-blood pressure, right? So we should not let your depression or anxiety go untreated either. It's not an embarrassment or an issue. It is a disease that requires medication, not unlike your blood pressure."

By removing the emotion from the situation, it allowed her patients to see other points of view and focus on the medical reason behind their conditions. Farah never got involved emotionally involved with her patients- that was the benefit of her "condition". However, sometimes she got frustrated with them because they were so emotional. There were days when she wanted to shout, "Get over it and move on!"

For as long as she could remember, Farah wanted to work in a palatial suite nestled on a high floor of a big office building with smoky glass windows. As a little girl, she remembered looking up at tall buildings in New York City and pointing to where her office would be. That is usually when her Aunt Janice would laugh and scold her. "Girl, your drunk ass mother never had a job more than two weeks before quitting or getting fired. You'll be doing good to get a decent job and keep it."

Farah reflected on her Aunt Janice who said that she would probably never become anything more than a drunk like her mother. Though she did in fact become a drunk, she also became a doctor. Farah was not just any old doctor. She had become a nationally known psychiatrist whose work in diagnosis and profiling had earned her quite a few awards and even more recognition. She had provided expert commentary more than a thousand times in her life. Law enforcement around the country sought her out for her profiling expertise.

There were many days when Farah wished her aunt could look up and see what a success she had turned out to be. She did not know whether Aunt Janice was looking up from the dirt or looking up from hell, but Farah was fairly certain that her aunt was not looking down from heaven. Her aunt spent an entire lifetime looking down on people – so it was only fitting that she spends eternity looking up at everyone now. At least that's how Farah saw it and that thought gave her great pleasure.

Farah smiled as she approached the sign "Farah Goodwyn & Associates, Mental Wellness". She was jolted by an empty waiting room when she walked into the office.

"Where is everybody? The nine o'clock crew is already back there?" Farah looked at her watch.

"Yup", replied her receptionist who sat behind the glass in perfect hair and makeup.

Quiana was the receptionist and office manager. Unable to find a job with her bachelor's degree in Biology and unable to get into medical school with low test scores, Quiana came to Farah with a proposal to run the office while she studied to retake the MCAT. That was ten years ago. She and Farah had developed a great working relationship and pseudo friendship, as well.

Quiana stood up behind the glass with her arms folded. She shook her head from side to side and gave Farah a "tisk tisk tisk" from her Viva Glam glossed lips. "Dr. Goodwyn, why is Kane in your office? What did you do?"

"Kane?" Farah tried to look confused. "Ooooohhhh the delivery guy? Yeah, nice dude."

"Dr. Goodwyn, don't try to BS me." She sniffed and looked around the room as if she were searching for a clue. "Yep, the stench is in the air. You are full of it, right now. So spill it!" Quiana folded her arms.

"It's nothing. We just met for coffee once."

"No way!" Quiana's voice carried through the office. Quiana was extremely professional but every now and then her ol' girl came out of nowhere.

"Quiana, lower your voice," Farah said. "The staff can hear you."

"Mmm Hmmm. You better watch out for that man. I know guys like that, Dr. Goodwyn. He's looking for a come up. Trust me."

"And how do you know that, Quiana?" Farah asked.

"Because he has never tried to get at me. He has been coming here two or three times a week for months now. Not one time has he asked me out for so much as a burger and fries. No offense, but the only thing you got on me is money." She ran both hands down her body and accentuated the curves that caused working class men to make comments as she walked through the streets of New York.

"Oh really?" Farah's eyebrows had risen to her hairline. "Quiana, You have yet to figure out that eventually you have to offer this world more than a big butt and smile."

Quiana rolled her eyes and let out an exasperated sigh. "Just be careful. I know guys like Kane who will do anything for a dollar. A man like that can easily see that you have more dollars than you have sense. I know you get your swerve on - but bringing it to the office? This time you better be careful. You feel me?"

"No. Not really," Farah quipped a bit irritated. "I know how to handle men. Besides, you're just mad. I think you like him." Farah grinned and winked at Quiana.

Quiana gave Farah a disgusted look. "Please! Just watch your back, Doc. There is something about him that just ain't right. I'm telling you." Quiana stomped her wedge heels and walked into the back office.

Farah was amused that Quiana thought a man could outsmart her. Farah studied human behavior for a living. She was shrewd and knew how to handle men of all types: white

collar, blue collar and no collar at all. In her opinion she had

plenty of dollars and plenty of sense, too.

It was a few minutes before nine o'clock, which meant

she had about two hours to spend with Kane. They had been

having great conversation and enjoyed a very nice lunch just

the day before, which she neglected to tell Quiana. She

switched out of her ballet flats into a pair of black sling back

pumps. Then she took a quick glance at her heels to make sure

they were not ashy.

Farah sauntered down the hall speaking to her staff of

social workers and psychologists along the way. She said

hello to each of the patients that were beginning their morning

sessions. Most of those people did not need full-blown

psychiatric treatment and never made it to the back office.

They had temporary life issues that needed to be worked

through like the death of a loved one or loss of financial status.

Farah's office only saw those patients that required

pharmacological intervention – the ones with true mental

disorders.

When she opened the double doors to her office, Farah saw that Kane's pants were draped over her desk chair and he was stretched across the couch in his boxers. There was a book in his hand. Kane loved to read. He especially enjoyed reading and debating psychology textbooks -which Farah found both ridiculous and alluring at once.

"Hey Lady. TGIF!" He laid the book on his chest and reached out for her. Farah grabbed his hand and smiled. He pulled her in for a warm, soft kiss.

"Good morning. You're out early," she said and kissed his nose.

"I miss you," he said with a chuckle.

"I just saw you yesterday," she scoffed.

"Too long," he said with a fake pout and poked out lip.

Farah sighed, kicked off her shoes, and cuddled on the sofa next to him. With her head on his chest she took a deep breath. He smelled freshly showered. Kane was such a well-kempt man. Not in the lights, camera, action way that Greg was put together. No one could compete with Greg's runway look and confidence, but Kane had a kind of manicured masculinity about him that Farah really appreciated.

"So, how's my baby today?" he asked.

"Not good actually."

He looked alarmed, "What's up?"

Farah started to explain the phone call they received this morning. A few sentences into her story about Bryann and the call, Farah noticed how uncomfortable Kane had become. He was fidgety and his chest moved rapidly up and down. "Are you okay?" she asked.

Kane spoke in a way that made Farah raise her head from his chest. His voice had a strange tone with a bit of a shake. "I'm fine." He motioned for her to continue.

His eyes were distant and Farah could see his mind was somewhere else. She looked into his eyes. "Something is bothering you, Kane. What is it?"

"I just hate to see you upset. We've been together nearly every day for the past month and you never mentioned to me that Bryann was adopted or that you were going through this."

"Well, it's not something I think about often. She's my daughter. And has been every day for almost fifteen years now. We just got the call this morning."

"You did?" he asked with a puzzled look.

"Yeah. Why?" Farah asked.

"I would think that maybe you should have stayed home with Bryann. How is she?"

Farah placed her head back on Kane's chest and sighed. "She doesn't know."

"You didn't tell her about the call?"

No. She doesn't know she's adopted?"

"What! Are you serious?" Kane pulled her face toward his.

"That's why I am so upset. I can fight off some irresponsible chick with guilt pangs after fifteen years. But telling Bryann - it will destroy her...and me."

"But I thought you had to tell your kids that they were adopted. I just read that somewhere. It's like some sort of law or something."

"No, in New Jersey the child has a right to unseal their birth certificate at age 18 to see who the birthmother is. The father is usually left out of it, of course. That's what's so frustrating about this. We adopted Bryann through international adoption to avoid this kind of thing. We got her from South Africa."

"South Africa?" Kane nearly threw Farah from his chest to the floor. "Are you sure?"

"Am I sure? What kind of question is that? Yes, I'm sure." Farah said.

"Well...I don't know. Never mind." Kane's lips twisted to one side with a deep frown on his face. "Man, this is crazy," he murmured. He pulled Farah in closer and rubbed her shoulders. His firm grasp felt so good that Farah imagined the tension escaping from her body and into his hands. She was so hot for Kane that whenever he touched her she felt an electricity shoot through her body and a fire between her legs. She had never known such physical attraction for a man before meeting him. It was understandable why some people believed in love at first site. If the feeling Farah had was what most people felt then no wonder so many people were crazy in love.

Farah was definitely crazy for Kane. He brought out a side of her personality that she had only heard about when her Aunt Janice told stories of her mother's adolescent days. Farah wanted to have sex with Kane so badly that her mouth was nearly watering. It was such a new feeling for her because she had nothing to gain from having sex with him except pleasure. It wasn't about money, status, power, or some thankless chore. Kane legitimately turned her on from the inside of her thighs to the top of her shoulders.

The thought of having to tell Bryann about the adoption was ripping Farah's heart out of her chest. She had thrown up her coffee that morning and still had knots in her stomach. However, all she wanted was for Kane to be inside her and make her feel better.

Ironically, Farah now understood what many people say about sex making them feel better. They say that when you are intensely attracted to someone, sex with that person makes you feel good emotionally and physically. Farah found this interesting since she never really felt "better" after sex as much as she felt accomplished and exercised.

Kane pulled Farah up on top of him then tossed her over on her back. He ripped down her panties and pulled her skirt up around her waist like he could not wait another minute for them to be together. Kane pulled her body towards him then bent her over the back of the couch with just enough force to be commanding but still made Farah feel safe and protected. He entered her easily but the width of his penis made the top of her vagina pop open. He was the biggest she had ever had. For the next twenty minutes they groaned and panted. It wasn't fairytale first time sex but it was damn good to Farah. She thought she almost had an orgasm. If Kane had moved a little more to the left it could have happened.

Though Farah "felt" better, her problems remained. This had always been her major rebuttal of emotion. It was utterly useless in accomplishing anything. Fear did not get you out of danger. Courage did not make you victorious. And love certainly did not make a relationship last. Emotion may be a compliment to action, but it was action that made things happen.

Aunt Janice had worked hard Farah's entire life to keep her out of the city and away from boys who would drive her crazy. According to Aunt Janice –who understood nothing of psychiatric illness - it was a man from Harlem that drove her mother to drink and into the depression that ultimately ended her life. Farah was married and in jeopardy of losing her daughter. Yet, she had sex on the office couch where she healed the world's problems, with a delivery guy from Harlem, nonetheless. Her aunt would say she had definitely gone crazy. Farah knew her Aunt Janice was spinning in her grave at that moment. She smiled at the thought.

The two lovers used the private washroom in Farah's office to freshen up after their long awaited session. Kane laid his chin on Farah's shoulder and smiled at her in the mirror like she was the only woman in the world. Maybe one of the reasons Farah adored Kane was because he made her feel special. He pursued her like he wanted nothing else in the world besides her.

After that first cup of coffee they did not have together he put on a full court press to get her attention. He sent sweet messages about missing her. At times she could hear the tears in his voice. He sent flowers, cards, candy, and love songs messages on her voicemail. He really over did it. But what she liked most was their conversation. They talked about everything from trashy reality TV to Freud's concept of Ego.

"That was good," Farah said.

"You know, it wasn't just about the sex, Doc." Kane whispered.

"It's always just about the sex - at first anyway." Farah turned around and kissed his soft moist lips. "My intellect is not what caused you to start pressing on me."

Kane's nervous laugh was followed by a big smile. "That's not true. You are a successful doctor. I knew that before I ever walked in and saw your face."

"Yes, but once you walked in you saw what I looked like then decided to pursue me. If I were a successful doctor who looked like Nanny McPhee you wouldn't be interested, now would you?"

Kane shrugged. "You don't know that. Every man wants to sleep with the nanny."

"We see how that worked out for Tiger Woods." They both laughed.

-5-

Quiana gave two quick knocks and entered the office without waiting for Farah to acknowledge her. It was a good thing that Farah wasn't still draped over the back of the couch with her skirt up to her collarbone. Quiana was already more than suspicious of Farah and Kane and since the two of them had been in the office for nearly an hour together, Quiana's suspicions were easily confirmed.

"Mmmm hmmm, just checking on y'all. It was kind of quiet in here. NOT!" Quiana said with a wry grin across her face. "I came in to let you know that the swirl is on the way up the elevator."

"The swirl?" Kane asked.

Liv and Callie were Farah's best girlfriends. One was black and the other was White so Quiana nicknamed them "the swirl". The analogy of "the swirl" actually was not the most appropriate because Olive, whom Farah called "Liv", was extremely fair with strawberry blonde colored hair, brown eyes, and freckles. She had the look that made white people think she was Caucasian with a bit of farmer's tan. Consequently, they said some pretty offensive things in her presence.

However, Black people could look at the bridge of her nose, full hips, and the fuzziness at the nape of her neck and tell she "had something in her." Both of her parents were African-American with deep caramel brown skin. She must have gotten the throwback gene. Either that or her mother had been lying to her father for forty years of their nearly perfect marriage.

Unlike her other affairs, Farah had kept Kane a secret from her girlfriends. That in itself said something about the nature of her relationship with him. She was not ready to explain the whole thing to them, especially to Callie, Detective Callista Piper, who was sure to make a federal case out of the fact that Farah kept it a secret.

"Oh great," Kane said. "I can finally meet the girls."

Quiana had annoyance in her voice. "Finally?" She paused. "This is going to be a mess, Doc." She rolled her eyes and walked out of the office.

"What's up with her?" Kane asked.

"I think she liked you," Farah said with a kiss on the chick. She looked at him directly in his eyes and smiled.

"What?" he quizzed.

Farah swallowed and did not say a word. She was sure Kane could tell by the look on her face that she was uncomfortable.

"C'mon Farah. Are you kidding me? You haven't told them about me yet?"

"It's only been a month," she said. "Besides there is too much on my mind right now." Farah put a stern look on her face to show that she meant what she said. Kane was not going to talk her into meeting the girls that day.

"Yes, but an amazing month. Right? We are more than just bed buddies. It took us a whole month to have sex."

"True." Farah nodded.

"I've never clicked with anyone like this before, Farah. I am just as surprised as you are. We are so different but so...so connected. The conversation is great. The sex is off the hook." Kane looked off into somewhere else.

"Yes, absolutely. I feel the same way. I plan to tell them. I do. I'm just a little preoccupied right now." Farah smiled and batted the dark eyes that had mesmerized Kane from the very beginning.

He conceded. Kane kissed her on the cheek and whispered a quick "Love you".

Farah understood the difference between "love you" and "I love you". When a man said, "Love you", it meant that he was really enjoying his time with you and he thought he might be falling in love with you. When he finally said, "I love you" it meant that he was ready. He was in love with you and wanted to make you his woman.

The notion that Kane thought he loved her was not a surprise at all to Farah. The thing that stunned her was that she believed that she loved him back. It was not something she needed to fake. Her vulnerability and words with him were true to the core. When she talked about her mother's death or her Aunt Janice's cruelty she left nothing out. She told it all to Kane and she had never done that before, not even with Greg.

The scariest thing for Farah was that, although the sex was incredible, it was secondary to the conversation and experiences she and Kane had shared. That was truly something new for her. She enjoyed every minute of it.

A couple of seconds later Liv and Callie pushed through the door like two rock stars walking the red carpet. They giggled and talked so loudly that Farah had to shush them. When Callie saw Kane she stopped and looked him up and down. "Hey! Hey! Wait a minute, Mr. Postman."

Kane looked back at Farah and chuckled, ignored Callie and walked out of the office. "Enjoy the day, ladies."

"Who was that?" Callie asked. She turned and watched Kane stroll down the office corridor. "And what can Brown do for me? Can I get him Thursday night? I have an opening in the roster."

"What I wouldn't give for an open day on the roster. Hell, I would take an open hour just to be by myself," Liv spouted before flopping on the sofa. "These kids are wearing me out."

Farah shook her head. "Olive Jones, you have a nanny, a housekeeper, and a gourmet meal service. How is it that you don't have an open hour for yourself? You look pretty open to me."

"So do you," Liv added with a snicker.

"Uh-hu," Callie cosigned. "What's up with you and your package boy?"

Farah raised a brow in false surprise. "What would make you say that? You spent three seconds with the guy." Farah started to wonder if her connection with Kane was obvious or if Callie was making assumptions based upon her cop consciousness.

"Number one, I am a detective." Callie said, "It's my job to notice everything. And number two, I may have spent three seconds with him but I've spent over thirty years with you and I know when you are smitten."

"Smitten? If only that were the case", Farah thought.

Callie's detective skills were not quite up to par on that assessment. Sweat still lingered across Farah's face like morning dew so she walked over to the window and flipped the switch to the ceiling fan. Then she directed her two girlfriends to sit down. She was still very warm from her sex session with Kane so she pulled a chair directly under the fan to cool down.

Over the next fifteen minutes, Farah explained to them the happenings of the last month or so. Why beat around the bush? So she dropped the bomb on them immediately. Besides it took some of the angst out of her chest by spitting it out all at once. Liv lounged on the couch with a goofy grin plastered on her face and the great Detective Callista Piper's mouth was gaped open at the first words that escaped from Farah's lips, which were, "He's my lover."

Farah knew she had broken the code. The girls were never, ever, under any circumstance to take a "lover." You had to spend time with a lover. You had to talk to a lover. A lover was a person with whom you developed a relationship.

Because they were married, Farah and Liv never took a lover. It did not make sense to do so unless they planned to leave their husbands, which neither of them did. Callie, who vowed to remain single, never took a lover because a lover became a boyfriend and a boyfriend became a husband. She was not interested in any of those three propositions.

For a moment the three of them sat in silence and looked around the room. They each waited for the other to speak. Farah had already said everything she was going to say so she simply waited for one of her best friends to respond.

The silence dragged on before Callie spoke. "Since when do we do 'lovers' ?" Callie got up and walked to the center of the room and spun around slowly in a full circle. "I'm a damn good detective. The washroom door is open, the center pillow on the sofa is backwards with the tag sticking out ..."

"Ugh!" Liv jumped up off the sofa.

"... and the fan hasn't completely eliminated the smell of hot sex in the room," Callie continued. "Which means you banged him at your office for the staff to hear and see. What are you thinking?"

"I guess I'm not thinking. Which is why this is so strange. He takes my breath away. I feel so much."

"Feel?" Liv asked.

"I know," Farah concurred. "Yes, I feel something for him. It's not something I've felt before so I can't say it's love but, whatever it is, I like it."

Callie frowned. "I knew when I walked in here that you two had been having sex. I smelled it before we even got to the door."

"Gross!" Liv squealed. "I don't smell anything. Thank God!"

"I'm trained to smell subtle odors in the air, Liv." Callie stared at Farah with such judgment in her eyes.

"Don't look at me like that, Callie. You came in here and wanted to put him in your open roster." Farah said sharply.

"Yeah Farah. I'm not married. I can do whomever I want, wherever I want, however I want. You are married to

Greg, who by the way will certainly make your life miserable if he finds out that you have actually been seeing someone. You have to stop this thing now."

Liv twisted her lips, "Callie, why are you acting like Farah has never cheated. Am I missing something here?"

"Aren't you always missing something? You smoke too much weed. " Callie said with irritation. "You are missing a bunch of coffee and lunches in public places. You missed multiple cell phone calls and voice messages. This is an affair. A relationship," Callie shouted. "You want to bang out the obscure Verizon guy or some young bartender in Punta Cana that you'll never see again? Fine. But this...this you have to stop."

"I don't want to stop," Farah said with a frown. She was more than vexed by Callie's attitude. "I thought you would want all the juicy details. Instead you are going to sit in judgment of me. You? The one-night-stand Princess Piper."

"Holy...she's gone mad!" Callie threw her hands in the air and sat down on the edge of the sofa. Not before cramming two pieces of chocolate in her mouth, which meant she was really upset because she never ate junk food.

"Well I think it's romantic," Liv said. "If you are happy, then I am happy for you. If you think you've found true love then go for it. Not many of us find it." Liv looked up at Farah with an "Uh oh" expression on her face. They both remained quiet.

Callie dropped her head into her hands. She had found love once. Callie was in love with a magnificent guy whom she met in the police academy. Everyone liked him so much because he was a perfect gentleman and a perfect fit for Callie. He and Callie kept their relationship a secret so they could remain partners on the force. That turned out to be a very bad idea. Her boyfriend was killed in the line of duty and Callie was there to see it unfold. She was unable to save him and he died in her arms.

Though it sounded a lot like TV, Farah never looked at those kinds of scenes the same again. After watching Callie battle that pain, there was nothing poetic about a lover dying in your arms. Farah continued to watch Callie drown her heart in one-night stands and meaningless flings. She wished she could heal her friend. But Farah vowed never to be Callie's psychiatrist. She was always her friend.

A few "unofficial" sessions with Callie over the years were in the form of "girl talk". Her problems started way before her fiancé died. Most of Callie's issues stem from growing up in the foster care system after being taken away from an abusive teenage mother. She was stuck in the system for six of her formative years before being adopted by an upper middle class black family that lived in a place Callie described as a "big house full of love"- a house that happened to be next door to Aunt Janice, a house Farah called a "big house cluttered with anger and misery". The girls lived very different lives, right next door to each other.

Callie was exalted as the only girl in the house. That notion had given her a dose of confidence twice the size of the Himalayas. She was also the only white person in her home and most of her social circle, which had given her a unique perspective into the thoughts and behaviors of different kinds of people. After watching her brothers constantly be profiled and hassled by police she decided to become a cop. Her deep insight into criminal behavior made Callie a very good detective. After her fiancé died, she shut down her emotion completely. This made her an exceptional detective.

"Love is a made up expression between two people who like each other at the moment." Callie told Liv. "You are a bleeding heart romantic. Life is real. Farah has a real life with a real husband and a real child, all of which she is putting at stake for a man she barely knows."

Liv interjected, "Yeah, what about that thing with Bryann we talked about this morning? Did you find out anything more?"

"We have our attorney working on it. I...I can't lose my little girl."

"Really? Because they way you are behaving it seems to me like you do want to lose her." Callie snapped. "If you don't lose her to this woman, then you may lose her to Greg when he finds out you've been cheating all these years."

"Callie, look. I get it. You think I'm getting in too deep. And you're right. But I can't help it. I think I love him. For real."

"But what do you really know about him to "love" him besides the fact that you have great sex and good conversation? So you can talk politics, hip hop, sports, current events and even shrink books. So what! If being more interesting than your husband is the criteria for love then you should be in love with that empty candy wrapper on the table."

Liv laughed in a burst. "That was just wrong. True, but wrong."

Farah was a bit offended and wanted to take up for Greg. Sure, he wasn't the most engaging guy on the planet, but what finance guy was?

"Maybe I should slow down a bit. Especially with everything going on with Bryann."

"Ya think?" Callie spouted.

Liv curled her nose, "Callie, ease up okay. It's not really fitting for a gypsy whore to sit on a high horse."

"Gypsy whore?" Farah and Callie said in unison.

"Yeah, you. Gypsy whore - going from place to place leaving your butt stains," Liv said with a smile.

"Stop it! Both of you stop." Farah shook her head. "Liv, I don't need you to defend me. I know I am a hundred percent wrong. And Callie, for real, ease up." Farah walked across the room and sat on her desk. She got a quick memory flash of the morning Kane walked into her office and she decided to engage him. She could have never guessed that her flirting would lead to a blow up between her and her best friends.

The girls never discussed the men they selected. They discussed the sex, the money, the expensive gifts, but never the actual guy. This thing with Kane had indeed gotten out of hand if they were having discussions about him.

Farah thought about all the men in her past. Though she was experiencing some feelings for Kane, she knew she could easily put herself back in complete control. Maybe Callie was right. Maybe she had gotten carried away with emotion. Go figure! She thought for a moment and decided to take her foot off the gas pedal with Kane.

Callie and Liv still bickered in the background of her thoughts. They continued to argue the concept of love. What is it? Who deserves it? Liv was going on and on about her love for Adam when Farah heard Callie say, "Please! Sasha Farce! If you are so in love, then why do you still fool around on him? Everyone knows how miserable you are with your life. Nobody knows better than the O'Neal's."

The O'Neal's lived in the subdivision with Liv and Farah. They owned a nearby liquor store. One day recently Mrs. O'Neal approached Farah. "Your friend Olive seems to come in a lot these days. You know she purchased over a case of vodka in a week. You should talk to her."

Farah snapped out of her thoughts. She looked across the room into the oval antique mirror on the wall. "Ladies, relax. I got this. I think it's time a settle down a bit."

-6-

Instead of slowing down, Farah's relationship with Kane intensified greatly. The more time they spent with each other talking and laughing, the more Farah begin to see herself with a different life. Being with Kane challenged everything she ever said or believed about love.

Kane and Farah pulled into the wooded area and he put a bandana over her eyes. They walked hand in hand a few feet down a rocky trail. She tried to ignore her watering, itchy eyes and the sneezing but it had become quite a task for her. She sneezed eight times in a row, nearly robbing her of breath. Just before Farah started to complain, Kane took the blindfold from her eyes and handed her a box of allergy & sinus medication with a small bottle of water.

"I thought you may have forgotten about my allergies," she said.

"Farah, baby, I've spent the last year learning every little detail about your life. I wouldn't bring you out here and not make sure you are protected. I love you girl." He kissed her.

She laughed. "Wow! Am I that bad that it feels like a year already? I think it's been more like six months, baby."

Kane forced a chuckle. "Actually, it has been seven months, a week and three days since we had coffee."

"Impressive." She opened her mouth wrapped her lips around his. "I love you."

The only thing in Farah's sight was a bunch of leaves and blooming flowers. She hoped there was more to this surprise than vegetation or else it was going to be a long day for Farah and her allergic rhinitis.

"You ready?" Kane asked.

She nodded even though she wondered why on earth he would bring her, with severe allergies, out to a floral garden in the heart of spring. Then Kane pushed through the wall of trees and that's when she saw the white sheet and picnic basket framed by tranquil blue water.

"How in the world did you find this?" She asked him with a smile spread so wide that it pulled her cheeks and squinted her eyes. "I love it!!" She squealed.

"Google. I searched bodies of water in Jersey," he said proudly. "I know you love the water. It keeps you calm. It helps you think."

"Yes, it does." She nodded and kissed him on the cheek. "But what do I have to be calm or think about?"

"Slow down. One thing at a time." Kane laughed.

The lake was gorgeous and gave the illusion of being secluded like the lakes you find in Ohio and Michigan. Even though she could still hear traffic that moved behind them, the thick wall of trees blocked Farah's view of the street. She could have easily been a million miles away from New Jersey.

An hour later Kane poured more sparkling grape juice into both of their glasses and then leaned in to kiss her bare shoulder. The sheet was wrapped around Farah like a toga, while Kane sat completely naked covered in sweat. He smelled like a sour dishrag now but it was just fine with Farah because he had worked hard to please her, and was successful in getting the job done.

Kane was the first man to ever bring Farah to orgasm - true orgasm. After that first time in the office, Kane had managed to knock it out of the park every time. Although Farah had gotten to be a pro at faking orgasm through the years with her feminine panting and howls, Kane brought her to a place where she could barely squeal because her body was paralyzed with pleasure. He could bring her to orgasm with his hand, finger, toe, tongue, and somehow this really bizarre thing with Farah straddled around his kneecap. He was amazing in the bed…on the floor, the balcony, and on the hood of the car, too.

She had grown to love him. She cried for him. Got angry at him. Became jealous over him. Felt pride in him. Kane Taylor had turned Farah from a wooden mannequin to a full grown, feeling, heavy breathing woman.

His voice dropped to just above a whisper. "Girl you know how much I love you," he said in between kisses on her neck and shoulder. "I want to spend the rest of my life with you."

She looked up at the clouds and thought about how much she loved him. "I love you too, baby," she said with a kiss.

If Farah had a quarter for every time some man had professed his love to her, she'd have a bank account that rivaled Warren Buffet's. In the last ten years - despite being married for the last sixteen - Farah had received four marriage proposals. She had keys to three different apartments in the city and had been given (and returned) seven luxury cars over the years. It was not a shock to Farah that Kane had fallen in love with her. She was in shock that she really loved him, too.

There was only one small cloud that floated in the sky above them. Farah thought it looked like a seashell on the water's edge. Kane thought it looked like a cinnamon roll with a toothpick in it. This was the story of their relationship. They could see the exact same thing and describe it the exact same way, yet come to two completely different conclusions.

It was a product of their different upbringing. Farah was a small town suburban Jersey girl who had never pumped gas a day in her life. Kane was a big city boy who was born in Detroit and moved to New York City before he could even remember. About a year ago he jumped over the Hudson to Jersey City when he started to work for the package delivery company. Essentially he spent most of his life in Harlem.

"So can I ask you something?" he said out of the blue.

"Ask me what?" Farah said.

"I said I want to spend the rest of my life with you, " he groaned and mumbled at the same time. "So I want you to leave your husband."

Farah smirked, "Kane...honey, that is not a question. You said you had to ask me something."

He frowned, "Dr. Goodwyn, I know it is not technically a question, but you know what I mean."

Whenever he called Farah "doctor" with great emphasis it was a way to criticize her intellect, which she quickly figured out was a coping mechanism he used to deal with her level of education and his lack thereof. Most days Farah ignored it but sometimes it really got to her.

"MISTER Taylor, you said you wanted to ask me a question. Can you clearly ask the question?" Farah knew her sharp and condescending tone bothered him just as she was bothered by the way he called her "Dr. Goodwyn".

"No." Kane rolled over onto his stomach and folded his arms beneath him. "No Farah," his muffled voice escaped.

For the next two minutes it was quiet. It was peaceful and as Farah gazed up at the sky she thought about how much she loved Kane despite their propensity to have little spats throughout the day. This had been a whirlwind few months and they had gotten so close that she wanted to spend every waking moment with him. He was not a perfect guy, but he was certainly perfect for her. Despite their differences in background, it worked for them. When she was with him, Farah was happier than she had ever been with a man.

She bent over and kissed the back of his head. "Sorry for being so snippy but you know I hate when you call me Doctor Goodwyn."

Kane raised his head from inside of his arms. His eyes were glassy. He asked, "Do you really love me, Farah?"

"Yes." She said it with strong conviction while locked into his eyes. "Do you have to ask?"

"Or am I just your little boy toy? Am I something to pass the time for you as an escape from your husband ?"

"Yes, I love you and yes you are my little boy toy." She rallied a smile that she thought he'd find amusing.

Farah was wrong. Kane went on to say, "I have invested months of my life in you. I truly believe we love each other. If we don't, tell me now."

Kane went on to admit that Farah turned out to be a completely different person than he thought she would be. "You are so sweet, Farah. You are such a good mom. You are not a snob and you don't use your status to make others feel bad. You are a good person and you don't deserve to be hurt in any way."

She frowned at him. "Oooooh-kay, not sure what all this is about, Kane. What do you mean I don't deserve to be hurt? Did you do something to hurt me?" Farah felt her defenses rise around her like a stone wall.

"No, I guess what I mean is that you deserve to be happy. I have grown to love you so much," he said. Then, Kane gazed at the clouds for a moment, his eyes watered. "Farah, I want you to leave Greg. But you have to do it because you really want to be with me. Not because I talked you into it."

"Talked me into it?" Farah twisted her face. "I guess you convinced me by making me so happy." She looked at him and he looked away. "Baby, it's only been a few months. Granted, the happiest months of my life but you know all that is going on right now with Bryann. It is just not a good time. But, if you are that serious, then I suppose we can start planning. I am meeting with Bryann's birthmother in a few days. Once I figure this out, we can be together. I promise."

"No," He took a deep breath. "You have to leave now...today. This week. Don't you love me?"

"I do." Farah pulled his chin around to look her in the eye. "We know we want to be together, right? So why rush it?

What's the big urgency all the sudden? We have our whole life ahead of us, Kane. Calm down. What's wrong?"

He nodded. "I just...I just want you to love me the way I love you. I want us to be together."

"So let's focus on that. Let's make a plan to be together. If that's what you want, let's do it." Farah gave him a reassuring smile.

Kane still did not believe that he had made his point to Farah. It was important for her to make this decision because she really loved him, not just because he asked her to make it. He cuddled with her under the blue sky with the smell of fresh water flowing through the air. There was no doubt in either of their minds that they belonged together. However, neither one knew how it would happen.

"I feel trapped," Farah said.

"So do I."

"Why do you feel trapped?" she asked.

"It's complicated." Kane looked at Farah and his eyes watered. He tightened his jaw. "Farah I never ever want to hurt you. I don't."

"So don't hurt me." Her heart started to beat a little harder. "What's going on Kane? Tell me."

"I can't...not now. But I will."

"Okay, now this is too much." Farah tightened the sheet around her waist and stood to her feet. "Kane Taylor, I am not playing with you. I have so much going on right now with Bryann, with work, with Greg. Don't play with me. Tell me."

Kane thought for a minute. "I never thought I would love you," he confessed. "When I met you...I mean, Quiana was right. I was out for myself."

Farah laughed, "Well Duh! You think I don't know that? You wanted to hit it, pimp a rich girl and brag to your boys. Kane, I know you didn't love me at first. Ummm, I didn't love you either. I wanted that boo-tay," she joked. "Plus you just smelled so darn good."

Kane opened his mouth to speak but Farah kneeled down and placed a finger over his lips. She wiped the sweat from his forehead. She tossed open her sheet and straddled him, pulled him close and put him inside of her. "Shhhhh, all

that matters is right now."

-7-

When the doorbell rang at 7:40 am Farah shouted, "Come in."

She had cracked the door open a bit already. Liv came over every morning while the nanny got her kids ready for school. When Liv stepped into the kitchen the smell of marijuana nearly knocked Farah over. Liv's eyes were glassy but not red and she had a diagonal smile stretched across her round, freckled face.

"Don't you think it's too early in the morning, Liv?"

"It's never to early for smoking when you live with Gladys Jones. She's on her soapbox about me this morning." Liv rolled her eyes in what seemed like slow motion. She mimicked her mother-in-law's raspy voice. "I guess they just don't make wives and mothers like they did in my day. Blah blah blah".

Farah laughed at her friend's impressive imitation.

"I love Adam more than anything but I swear... if I had spent any time with his mother before we got married...I would not have married him."

"Yeah right." Farah pursed her lips. "From the moment Greg introduced you guys you were hooked."

"Well, I never would have allowed her to come live with us. Her ass would be in a home for the elderly right now - and not a nice one. I'd put her in one of those places where people put parents when they don't want to be bothered with them."

Liv pushed past Farah and went straight to the refrigerator. She poured herself a half glass of orange juice and took a seat. Just when Farah thought that Liv might actually enjoy a glass of orange juice in the morning, she pulled a Gucci flask from her pocket. "Screwdriver?" she offered with an air toast.

"I see," Farah said with a shake of her head. "So you know today's the day I meet Bryann's birth - ". Farah couldn't bring herself to finish the word. Her eyes stung and the butterflies had returned to her stomach.

"So how are you feeling?" Liv asked. Before Farah could say anything further Bryann bounced down the stairs with a sour look on her face.

"What's wrong with him?" Bryann asked and thrust her thumb towards the stairs.

"I assume by 'him' you are referring to your father." Farah paused for moment. "Nothing is wrong with him. Why?"

Bryann explained, "He's in warp speed on the elliptical." Greg was an avid exerciser but warp speed meant that he was aggressively attacking his workout. Bryann continued, "He's got the TV on... with sound. He's flipping through his iPad and listening to his iPhone with headphones in?"

There was no doubt that he was bothered by the events to come. Whenever Greg overloaded on sensory stimulation like iPhone, iPad, and Apple TV at once, it meant he was drowning out the "noise" in his head. Whenever he did not want to think he made the surrounding environment so intrusive that he could not think if he tried. Greg was a stoic but when it came to Bryann his emotion rushed out like rough rapids.

Farah remembered the first time Greg held Bryann in his arms. He looked mesmerized, completely stupefied. The two of them, father and daughter, seemed to be studying one another. Bryann stared right into her daddy's face and Greg was just toast for his little girl. It was a beautiful moment, Farah recalled, that was interrupted by Greg's mother declaring, "She even looks to be a mixed breed. Maybe you two can actually pull this off."

Fourteen years later, Farah smiled as she watched Bryann hover over her fruit bowl and yogurt. Thoughts of the precious little girl flooded Farah's mind. Sitting at the breakfast table, Farah caught a glimpse of the beautiful baby girl they brought home on a twenty-one hour flight. Bryann was such a good baby. She slept most of the way and even at just days old had flashed a smile at the flight attendant. The lady across the aisle said it was gas but Farah and Greg knew it was a sign of happiness from their new bundle of joy.

"Sweetie, is that all you are going to eat before school?"

"Yeah, I'll be fine." Bryann popped up from the table, grabbed her backpack, and gave Farah a gentle kiss on the cheek. "Love you, mom."

That was Farah's precious little girl...fully medicated. When Bryann took her medication she was a completely different young lady. She was an absolute joy - smart, sweet, focused. In the moments when she was not compliant with her meds, Bryann lived a life beyond what Farah could bare to think about as a mother. As a psychiatrist, Farah knew all too well the kinds of things mania could produce in the lives of young girls - reckless sex, irresponsible spending, and excessive drug use. For many young women, one manic episode could produce irreparable damage to physical, emotional, and financial health.

Bryann gave Liv a kiss on the cheek, too. "Bye." She skipped towards the door and turned back. "Oh, and I can get you a deal on some better weed. That junk you have smells weak."

Liv's eyes popped open and they were no longer glassy. Bryann's acknowledgement knocked her sober. "Oh sweetie, I have cataracts. My doctor prescribes this for me."

Cataracts? Farah looked at Liv with an expression that said "Are you serious?"

Bryann laughed aloud. "I think you mean glaucoma, Auntie Liv," she said. "I can let you sample some of my stuff later." And just that quick the three minutes of innocent memories Farah had of her darling baby girl were gone.

As Bryann slammed the front door, Greg came down stairs drenched with perspiration and body spray. His dark hair was soaked and sticking to his apple colored face. He looked like a "Men's Health" cover. He was undeniably hot and sexy as any man on the planet. Farah still felt no attraction to him at all.

He threw the towel around his neck and grabbed a protein shake from the refrigerator. "Hello wife. Hello best friend's wife."

Greg bent down and lay his lips firmly on top of Farah's in a way that should have made her panties fall to the floor. "So today's the big day, huh?" Greg said as if it were a sincere question.

Farah looked back at him without answering and he continued to talk as if he were trying to convince himself. "Well, this will be over in no time. Despite New Jersey's law, the adoption took place in South Africa and those laws apply to this case. Alan said this woman hasn't a leg to stand on. "

****

As it turned out Bryann's birthmother had two very nice legs to stand on. She was built like a fashion model. When she walked into the room it was like Farah was put in a time machine to the future. For nearly fifteen years, Farah was convinced that Bryann looked much like an emulsion of Greg and herself. It turned out that Bryann looked exactly like her birthmother, who had the same killer body and bewitching grey eyes. Farah looked at Greg but he did not seem at all affected. How could he not see those double D's in 3D coming through the door?

Farah could not take her eyes off of the woman. The woman was absolutely striking - just like their daughter. In all of Farah's dreams Bryann's birthmother was an old, ragged-looking woman whose face was a canvass for her hard living and poor choices. In Farah's mind, the woman had crooked, rotten teeth. Instead Farah and Greg were greeted by a perfectly straight, bright white smile that glowed as the woman walked across the room. She extended her hand to Farah first.

"I'm Riley Briggs. Nice to meet you."

Farah grabbed her hand with a firm, but friendly shake. There they were, Bryann's two mothers. Farah really wanted to hate this woman on sight but somehow she couldn't do it. Riley was the vessel that brought her little girl into the world and changed her life forever. In Riley's eyes, Farah could see her daughter smiling two decades in the future. Much to Farah's surprise, her heart was filled with warmth and something akin to love.

Kane had made her a big emotional mess. It seemed that every little thing evoked emotion in her now. She cried when the news showed missing children. She felt tingly inside when her patients told stories of their newfound happiness. Now, here she was faced with an adversary and all she felt was some sort of gratitude and kindness.

Greg, on the other hand, was ready for battle. He had a scowl stretched across his face and reluctantly shook Riley's hand. When Riley walked back to the other side of the conference room Farah leaned over to lighten his mood. "She has a great butt."

"My only concern with her butt is to kick it right back where she came from and out of our lives," Greg said without the slightest hint of humor. Before Riley and the arbitrator could sit down completely Greg blurted out, "What is it you want? Money?"

The angelic eyes that had previously eased Farah's angst now morphed into dark piercing daggers. "Look!" she said. "I tried to come in here with the right attitude, but we can do this however you like. Trust me Mr. Goodwyn, you don't want to mess with me."

A sound, something between a gasp and a sigh, flew from Farah's lips. The arbitrator's face had turned nearly orange. The room became antagonistic in a snap and the prior warmth in Farah's heart turned to fear.

"Mrs. Briggs..." Greg began.

"It's Ms. Briggs. I did not take my husband's name," she said.

"You're married?" Farah asked.

"She's going through a divorce." Greg answered. Apparently he had more information than Farah did. Greg had a wily smirk across his face. "And why doesn't your husband want to be here?"

"My estranged husband is not Lila's father," Riley said.

"Who the hell is Lila?" Greg growled. "Our daughter's name is Bryann. Bryann Goodwyn. It's the only name she's ever known."

Farah was certain she was going to vomit right in Greg's lap. Her heart started pounding and a full blow sweat broke out from her scalp. She wanted a real drink...not wine either - hard liquor - and not diluted in some fruity concoction filled with ice and an umbrella. Farah needed a half of a glass of Jack Daniels. Straight up! But she knew that if she took one drink it could change her life.

She tried to pull herself together but Farah felt the tears welling in her eyes. The pool blurred her vision. Before she could manage anything the water from her eyes poured down her face. She felt gaping loss inside of her. It felt like someone had pulled a chunk out of her - like lifting out the middle piece out of jigsaw puzzle.

Suddenly Farah had a memory of being in a room full of people staring at her and they were all crying. Farah remembered her Aunt Janice picking her up from a pile of toys in the center of the floor. She held Farah with her and stood behind a microphone to speak to all the crying people. Farah could see her grandparents in the front row looking nearly lifeless. She reflected on the words she heard. "This little girl will be alright. Each of us, as friends and family, will ensure her life is full of happiness and free from the pain that has created this situation. It was pain and foolishness that brought us all here today," her Aunt Janice said into the microphone that day. The crowd of people nodded in agreement.

After nearly forty years, Farah remembered her mother's funeral. Facing the loss of her daughter jolted her subconscious into a mode of loss and despair. She felt like her heart was going to stop beating at the moment she heard Riley call Bryann by another name.

"I'm sorry. You're right Mr. Goodwyn." Riley grimaced. "From now on, I will call her Bryann."

"Because that's her name," Greg asserted.

He leaned into the conference table with his arms stretched out and palms slammed down on either side of him. "Look, our daughter doesn't even know that she's adopted so you can understand how you don't fit into our family equation."

Riley and Greg went back and forth while the arbitrator took notes and nodded with pleasure at the seemingly intelligent and respectful dialogue. Farah breathed in and out through her nose to keep from gasping for air. Her throat was so dry that it started to become sore and her head spun from the back and forth rhetoric between Greg and Ms. Briggs.

After an hour of debate the arbitrator held up his hand to make a statement. "Well folks, it doesn't look like we will come to an agreement here. I'd advise that you both retain counsel at this point and we will move forward with official proceedings."

Riley stood to her feet and reached out for Farah's hand. When Riley tried to release the handshake Farah held on to her hand. "Ms. Briggs, we have given Bryann a really good life just as you wanted for her when you offered her for adoption. She has quite a few problems and disrupting our family life could be detrimental to her health. You are putting my daughter in jeopardy by destroying the only family life she's ever known."

Farah's voice was just above a whisper and her tone was drenched in a plea for compassion with a toughness that only a mother could muster.

Despite Farah's attempt, Riley's face took on a sneer that looked like she had been waiting years to say what came next. "Dr. Goodwyn, family is built on love, trust, and years of beautiful memories. Little ol' me can't destroy that. So, if your family is destroyed, I'm quite sure it is not because of my desire to visit with my daughter. " Her lips were covered in condescension.

"She's not YOUR daughter!" Greg shouted.

Riley's head snapped toward Greg and she spoke through clenched teeth. "I conceived her. I carried her. I birthed her. She most certainly IS my daughter." Then she turned toward Farah and her voice rose to nearly a shout. "To be clear, Dr. Goodwyn. I don't give a damn about the life you've built pretending to be my daughter's mother. You say you love her, but you aren't even truthful with her."

The mother bear snapped in Farah. "Bitch, don't you question the love I have for my daughter. As the woman that gave her away, you have no right. You have no idea all that we have been through as a family. Bryann is sick - and now I see why." Farah's voice nearly shook the pictures on the conference room walls.

Riley took a deep breath and let out a long sigh. "Well, well, well. She does actually have a spine.... I'm impressed. And here I thought you were just a doting, devoted, suburban wife with no mind of your own."

She sneered at Farah. Farah looked straight into her eyes and returned fire for fire. Farah was feeling all sorts of emotion for the first time. She thought she had killed her expression of anger long ago in those days of living with Aunt Janice. She vowed never again to let anyone have control over her behavior by provoking her emotions. But, in this case it was very much warranted. If Ms. Briggs wanted a fight with Farah, she was going to get it.

Riley saw that Farah was as cold and stone-faced as she was. She said to her, "Dear Dr. Goodwyn, I've made my mistakes. Nobody is perfect. And those that claim to be usually have full skeletons in their closets- two hundred and six bones." Riley leaned in and dropped her hands to the table. "You are keeping secrets, doctor." She tossed her hair over her shoulder. "And secrets have a way of coming out eventually. Trust me. I know."

Farah leaned in even closer to Riley. "I'm sure you do. And wherever you read that there are two hundred six bones in a human skeleton," Farah paused. "Quite impressive... I suggest you turn to the chapter on how many muscles there are in the human body. Because I plan to use every single one to fight you and keep you away from my daughter."

Riley scoffed. "You have some time before I win my first visit. I suggest you tell her the truth before then. The whole truth."

Farah stood unmoved with her chin slightly raised like she was bracing for a left hook. Riley looked like she wanted to punch Farah in the face. And Farah certainly wanted to slap Riley. There was something very devious about Riley, nearly wicked. But Farah had some internal wickedness of her own to dish out if it meant protecting her family.

Riley smirked as she turned to walk out of the conference room. "I'll be seeing you."

Farah quickly caught up with her. "You certainly will," Farah agreed. "Oh, and Ms. Briggs...

"Yes," Riley turned toward Farah.

Farah leaned in and glanced across the room at Greg who was apparently speaking with the attorney on the telephone. Farah and Riley locked eyes and both could feel the breath of the other.

Farah whispered between barely opened teeth "...I don't have a skeleton in my closet. I have a full cemetery of bodies - with one open grave left for you."

Riley chuckled.

"Laugh now," Farah said.

Riley smiled pleasantly, "I will. And I think I'll have the last laugh too."

Farah stood with anger building in her chest as Riley walked away. She looked back at Greg who was still on the phone shouting at the attorney. He mind quickly went back to Aunt Janice's words at her mother's funeral. "It was pain and foolishness that brought us here today."

-8-

It had been almost three years of meticulous planning but the day had finally come and Riley had gotten to meet the people who adopted her daughter. The joy she felt fifteen years ago when she first saw the two pink lines on the pregnancy test was quickly doused by the father of her child. At the time Kendall had a wife and Riley was planning a wedding of her own. So Kendall sent her to South Africa for the last six months of her pregnancy and she gave the baby up for adoption. She quickly got over the pain of that decision and moved on with her life.

Riley came from a long line of unscrupulous women that did whatever it took to get what they wanted -- which was usually a man. Most women were driven by their hearts in relationships. Riley chose to use her brain...and her lady parts, which was precisely how she was going to get Kendall away from his wife.

Riley's relationship with Kendall was passionate and very public. Everybody knew who she was, except Kendall's wife Lorraine. Until that dreadful day -- the day Riley saw Kendall and his wife together in the hospital. Lorraine's protruding belly sent Riley over an edge of vicious rage. She told Lorraine everything. She had over a decade of "love making and trip taking" for Lorraine to hear about -- including the baby Kendall had forced her to give away.

That day, Kendall vowed to be a loving faithful husband to his wife and a good father to their unborn child. Yet, within three weeks, he and Riley were back together.

The night Lorraine went into labor, Kendall was in Riley's bed. When Lorraine's daughter took her first step, Kendall and Riley were cruising the Mediterranean. Riley felt as important as ever in Kendall's life until the day he blew her off for his daughter's 3-year old dance recital. That's when she felt her grip loosening to "daddy's little girl". Lorraine had gotten smart and started to use the little girl to keep Kendall away from Riley. That's when Riley came up with the plan.

She grabbed her cellphone from the kitchen counter and commanded, "Call Kendall." She flopped down on the sofa. It was worth it to Riley to rent a place in New York until this whole ordeal was finished. Riley was a bit appalled by the money she had to spend on renting such a tiny apartment downtown, but she saw it as an investment in her future.

Kendall answered the phone on the first ring, "Where are you?" he asked with panic in his voice.

"I'm in New York City."

"New York? What the hell are you doing in New York City?" He grunted like he didn't want to hear the answer. After all, Riley always acted out to get his attention when she was angry with him.

"I found our daughter," Riley said faking a whimper. "I found her Kendall." There was silence on the line. She couldn't even hear him breathing. "Hello?".

"Yeah, I'm here," he said.

"So?" she asked.

"So, what? Oh, you want my opinion now? How could you do this without discussing it with me first? This is so....so…so damn Riley."

"What does that mean?" she asked.

It sounded to Riley as if Kendall had pounded the phone on the wall. "I give you everything! Everything! I give you all my love and most of my money. Why are you doing this? Is this some kind of retaliation against my daughter?"

Riley stood to her feet as if she were getting in Kendall's face. "This IS your daughter we are talking about Kendall, remember. You have two daughters. I am spending my life with you. I don't date other men. I don't screw other men. What about me? How am I going to have kids?" she asked with a whine that even she wasn't certain whether or not it was sincere. "I want children, Kendall."

"Riley please stop the drama! Is this because Stormy is pregnant again? We've been together for nearly twenty years. I've never heard you say you wanted children."

Riley screamed and real tears fell from her eyes. "That's because you made me give mine away, Kendall! And then you let Lorraine have your child. How could you do that to me? Have you ever thought about how it makes me feel to see you smile at the thought of your daughter with Lorraine knowing that our daughter, your first child, was out here alone."

Kendall got quiet on the phone and Riley knew she had him thinking. Though she was tough and calculating, the tears and pain she felt at the moment were very real -- much to her own surprise. She was empty with half a man and no children and she just realized that it was starting to hurt. She took a deep breath. "You know what Kendall, go be with your family. I don't need you."

"But Riley..." he shouted before she hung up the phone.

If up to Riley, Lorraine would not have one more moment of happiness with Kendall. The one way to ensure turmoil in their marriage was to find the daughter she and Kendall had given away. After searching for almost three years, she had done that.

She went to the bar and poured herself a shot of tequila. In her frustration she yelled into the phone. "Call Stormy!"

"The temperature is seventy-two degrees. It is not expected to storm," the robotic voice responded.

"Call Stormy damn it!" Riley yelled again.

"Calling Stacey Anderson" the voice responded.

"NO!" She yelled. Then Riley took a deep breath and calmed her voice. "Call Stormy," she said calmly in a stern voice that hid her agitation.

"Calling Stormy," the voice echoed.

Her cousin answered the phone on the first ring, "Where are you?"

"Why is everyone in such a panic?" Riley asked.

Stormy sighed, "Riley, we haven't heard from you in over a week. That's never a good sign. You need to call Kendall. He's going bananas."

"Whatever. I just got off the phone with him. I'm done." Riley said.

Stormy laughed. "Yeah right. I've heard that about a million times."

"I'm serious. Anyway...I have to tell you something."

"Uh-oh, what did you do?" Stormy asked.

"Why do you just automatically assume I did something?" Riley got a bit indignant.

"You can't be serious right now, Riley. Just tell me what's going on." Stormy said.

"I found my daugh..."

"What! That's great!" Stormy cut her off mid syllable with huge excitement. "But how? When? Where?" Then, she paused for moment and her voice changed from excited to skeptical. "Wait...why?"

"Why? Because she's my daughter and I love her."

"Riley, I know you. What's going through your mind? I've only heard you speak of this child one time in your life."

"What the hell is going on with everybody? Why can't I just want my child back? Women throw their children in dumpsters and come back for them. Maybe I have realized my mistake and now I have set out to correct it."

Stormy remained quiet.

Riley continued, "I found out that she has been in America this whole time. She was adopted by a couple from here. Can you believe that?"

"Where is 'here'? Where are you?" Stormy questioned.

"New York City. Well, she actually lives across the river in New Jersey but it's the same thing. I met the people who adopted her today. A white man and a black woman. She's a doctor. A shrink."

"The irony," Stormy said inside of a sigh.

"Whatever!" Riley moaned. "Anyway, I'm fighting for visitation and I'm going to get it."

"Why on earth would anyone just grant you visitation after all these years? I think you are being a bit presumptuous." Stormy warned.

Riley laughed. "Oh cousin dear, when have you ever known me to be presumptuous? I can be pretentious, precipitous, and predaceous. But never presumptuous. I have it all figured out."

"And here it comes, " Stormy declared. "Here comes the plan ladies and gentlemen."

"I have some help," Riley said.

"From who?"

"Zo."

"Zo?" Stormy laughed. "How on earth did you get him to help you?"

"I'll tell you later. But the real problem is that Lorraine is trying to get Kendall to move to California so that little girl can be near his parents. She's playing the grandparent card." Stormy remained quiet but Riley heard the disapproval in her silence. "She isn't the only one who has a child for Kendall's parents to love. It's time they met their first born granddaughter."

"Riley…"

"Nope. Save your breath. I'm doing this. It's already in motion. There are always casualties in war. I'm battling for Kendall and unfortunately the Goodwyn family is collateral damage."

"So, let me guess. You seduced the father."

"Nope. He's a no nonsense finance guy of sorts and he absolutely loves his family. After watching him for a few days I knew I had no chance of that."

"That's a first." Stormy scoffed.

"Tell me about it. I had to check my ego too." Riley said, "At first I thought he was gay."

"Of course you did," Stormy said. "So, if you can't sleep with him, what else are you going to do? Your tricks are a little limited outside of that. I mean, if you don't really want to have a relationship with the girl, why don't you find another way to keep Kendall from moving to California?"

"There is no other way!" Riley screamed. "Don't you think I've tried to think of other things? This is it. I've got to get our daughter back."

"But how?"

"I can't tell you." Riley said.

"Yeah. You won't tell me because you know it's probably awful and you don't want me to try to stop you."

"Exactly...anyway I have another call. I'll call you in a few days with an update." Riley looked at her phone and smiled. She swiped the button to change calls. "Hey babe!"

"What's up?" The voice on the other end sounded deep and groggy. "You called me?"

"Yep. How are things going?"

"I need to talk to you about that...in person. Can you meet me?"

"No, I can't. I had that awful meeting today and I'm drained so just spit it out." Riley demanded.

"Well, I don't think I can help you. Your daughter looks happy, healthy and loved."

"I don't give a damn if she looks like a walking Disneyland! I need you to do what I asked you to do. Stay with her and let me know her every move."

"I'm telling you she's a typical, but troubled, teenager. She goes to school. Hangs with friends. Smokes a little weed and goes home."

"And what about her mother?" Riley asked.

"I'm making progress but..."

"But what?

The voice on the phone sounded disgusted. "Look, you are my girl and I love you. But I can't do this for you. Not this."

"Why not Zo?"

"From what I can see they are good people," he said. "They are a close family. It's going to be impossible to get the girl away from them."

"Close family? Please! A wife that repeatedly cheats on her husband, a husband that works so much he barely notices does not constitute a good family." Riley scoffed.

"Look! You're on your own. I'm not risking this for you."

"Not so fast, my friend. There is the little notion of $5700 I paid to those people for you." Riley tapped her fingernails on the back of the phone. "You owe me. That debt transferred from them to me," she said. "And trust me, I'm worst than they could ever be. They would have cut off your legs. I'll cut out your heart. Don't test me, Zo."

"You're evil," he said. "This is not going to work, Riley. You can't take a child from the parents and expect that child to love you."

"I don't need the little girl to love me, you idiot!" Riley yelled. "I just need her to know I am her mother and Kendall is her father."

"So wait...this is about Kendall?" There was a loud exhale through the phone. "There it is... I knew there was more to this. So you are trying to destroy two families. You're a terrible person."

Riley's anger flared. "Don't judge me. You try to make your way without a father. Go visit you mother in a mental institution every week. Then tell me what kind of person I am. I have been by myself for most of my life. So I think I am doing okay considering. Don't you?"

"Look, I'm sorry. I didn't mean it like that," he said.

"I don't care how you meant it. I don't care how you feel. You better find a way to hijack my daughter from these people. You better get that man to leave his wife. You better bust up that family. Or else...you will wish those boys from

around the way get a hold of you before I do."

-9-

Farah and Kane had been enjoying themselves openly for months. They ate in popular restaurants, hung out in trendy places, and attended public events. Farah did not feel the need to hide her relationship with Kane, though she felt that they needed to use appropriate discretion not to exposure her affair to Greg. Over the months, she had come to terms with her love for Kane. He had been a huge support throughout the ordeal with Bryann. So, Farah felt it was time to start showing him her commitment to the future.

"So what's my surprise?" Kane asked.

"If I tell you it's not a surprise, right?"

"Well, you've been talking about it for over a month so I'm ready to be surprised."

Farah leaned into the driver. "Make a left up here at the light, please."

She watched Kane's brow raise the way it does when he's perplexed by something. Then the left crease around his mouth started to dimple, which meant he had some anxiety about the situation. She proudly believed that she had managed to learn every nuance of his personality.

Farah held her breath until the driver stopped the car in front of a beautiful newly renovated apartment building. "We'll be back down in about an hour," she said.

"Who lives here?" Kane said.

Farah didn't answer but motioned for him to follow her. "A friend of mine owns this with his girlfriend. They haven't moved in yet so I figured..." She winked.

Kane chuckled, "Oh okay. I'm liking this surprise so far." He swatted her on the backside.

Before they could get out of the elevator they had their hands all over each other. The passion between Kane and Farah was something she had never felt before. She wanted him every moment of every day. She wanted to smell him, kiss him, wrap her legs around his naked waist.

They arrived at the 41st floor and Farah squealed in excitement. She ran down the hallway with Kane playfully chasing behind. They both giggled like teenagers. When they arrived at the apartment door, Farah looked at Kane and pushed the door open. "Welcome home."

Kane swallowed and his eyes widened. Farah stood next to him. The view was amazing. It was a clear day and you could nearly see the entire stretch of Central Park. It was a decent size apartment and full of light. So it made it look a little bigger.

"This is our place," Farah squealed. "I bought it for you...for us."

"You what? Are you crazy?" Kane shouted.

Farah was taken aback, "I thought you'd be happy."

"Farah, what if Greg finds out about this. What about Bryann?"

"That's why I bought it for us. So we have our own safe place. For us to create our memories and start living our life."

"No baby, no." Kane wrapped his arms around her. "You can't jeopardize your life like this. You need to wait until after the court date."

"But, I thought this is what you wanted. I thought you wanted us to be together."

"I do. But not like this. We need to wait."

"What?" Farah looked at Kane with a frown. "We love each other, right?" She said in a whisper.

He sat on the carpet and pulled her down to his lap. "Yes. Yes we do. I love you more than anything, Doc. But I also know that you love your daughter. He paused. "From what you told me, this woman sounds like she could be big trouble. Don't risk it."

"I can handle Riley Briggs," Farah said. Kane winced at the name. He grabbed his head with two hands. "What in the world is wrong with you?" Farah asked.

"Nothing. Nothing." He lifted her from his lap. "Let's just go grab something to eat and talk about this some more."

Farah laughed, "I have the only man on the planet who likes to talk." Farah kissed him. "That's why I love you."

"Farah, let's get out of here," Kane said sternly.

Her face turned downward. "Okay fine."

They went back down the hallway and into the elevator. The mood had shifted from the playful, loving, youthful banter to solemn, hidden disappointment in just minutes.

Kane and Farah got into the car and rode downtown in complete silence. Farah looked out the window with tears in her eyes. She regretted ever opening up to Kane. She thought back on everything her Aunt Janice had ever told her about Black men. She thought about all the things many women had said over the years about a Black man's inability to commit to a monogamous life. There was a hole forming in Farah's heart.

Meanwhile, Kane looked out the opposite window with a huge lump in his throat. He could not decide what to do. He wanted to be with Farah badly, but he also wanted what was best for her family at the moment. He did not want he to lose her daughter. He turned toward her but she never turned away from the window. "Baby?" he said and reached out for her hand.

She pulled away. "Kane, please don't speak to me right now."

He dropped his head and went back to looking out of the window.   They arrived at the seaport and Farah wouldn't get out of the car. Kane waited outside for a moment before opening her door. "Get out."

"Don't tell me what to do." She folded her arms like an eight year old.

"Farah, get out of the car," Kane demanded, but with a gentleness that almost made Farah smile.

"No!"

He sighed. "Baby, please get out of the car. Let's go talk."

"I don't want to talk. I want to go home to my husband."

"Wow!" Kane shook his head but didn't move from his position holding the car door. "So, that's what it looks like when you are hurt?"

"I'm not hurt. I'm angry..." Farah continued. "...With myself. I'm angry with myself for loving you."

Kane squatted down beside the car door. "Baby, will you please just take a walk with me so we can talk."

"I want to go home, Kane."

"Okay. Okay. But just take a walk with me first." Kane begged.

Farah reluctantly got out of the car. She was irritated by her inability to resist Kane. As much as she wanted to leave him standing with the Brooklyn Bridge at his back, she grabbed his hand and they started walking.

He leaned over and kissed her on the cheek. "I love you too much to rush you into this."

"You're not making any sense, Kane. You were the one who asked me to leave Greg. You said we needed to do this quickly."

"That was months ago." Kane said.

"So, you changed your mind?" Farah asked.

"No, not at all. But now you are in the midst of a heated custody battle with this...this crazy woman. Now is not the time." Kane picked up a rock from the ground and threw it into the river. "You are so damn impulsive." He took a deep breath. "I wish you would have discussed this with me first."

"I wanted to surprise you."

"Well, I'm surprised." He smiled at her.

Kane put his arms around Farah as the cool air blew Farah's hair into her face. Kane gently tucked it behind her ear just like the first time they had met at Starbucks. He had no idea how this whole thing was going to resolve. Kane would have to figure out how to keep Farah from being so impulsive and how to keep her in his life forever at the same time. He looked into her eyes and his eyes stung with fear.

"What's wrong?" She asked.

"I love you so much, Farah. I hope you always remember that."

"I will," she said and passionately kissed Kane. They started to make out right there on the pier for everyone to see.

She did not care. She moved his hand down to the small of her back and he slid his hands under her blouse. The touch of his hands on her skin was sizzling.

They went back to the car and ordered the driver to "take a walk". The windows were just slightly tinted but they didn't care. Farah straddled Kane in the back seat and gave him everything. Her breath. Her heart. Her life. The car got so warm that they were forced to put the windows down a little. Anyone walking by could see that she was on top of him but not exactly what they were doing. It looked like they were just making out like teenagers but they were making love.

Several people walked down the side street with a whistle. One couple started kissing after watching Farah and Kane for a moment. A love like theirs was the envy of all to see. Farah was happy. Kane was happy. Farah believed that in time they would be together. For the first time in her life, she would not have to fake emotion. She was in love.

****

By the time Farah got back to her house, Greg was already at his wine club meeting and Bryann was out with her friends. Though the day started out rough, Farah was still walking on the clouds. It had only been three hours since she and Kane were together but she missed him already. She grabbed her phone to call him.

"Hey boy!"

"Hey baby! What's up? You miss me?" Kane asked.

"Yes!"

"I miss you too," he said.

"So what are you doing tonight?" Farah asked.

"I'm going to dinner with my parents. Just hanging out with them."

"That's nice. You are such a good son." Farah smiled into the phone. "You're such a good man."

Kane paused for a moment. "Thanks," he said. "I'll call you in the morning."

Farah hung up the phone and decided it would be a perfect night to catch up on her DVR recordings. She quickly took off her clothes, put on some grey yoga pants and a white tank top. She plopped on the sofa with a bottle of water and a bowl of potato chips. Just as she settled in the doorbell rang.

"Liv!" Farah scoffed. "Come in!" The door didn't open. Farah sighed and got up out of her comfy place. She sauntered to the door, talking as she opened it. "I said come in."

There was no one at the door but there was an envelope on the ground. It was addressed to Greg. There was no stamp and it wasn't in a courier envelope, just a plain manila envelope and it wasn't sealed. She picked it up and went back inside. Then she opened the door again to look around. There was not a single car on the street.

Farah tossed the envelope on the kitchen counter and went back into the family room to settle in again. Just as she sat down, she looked back toward the kitchen. Suddenly she got curious. She wanted to know what was in that package so she went back to the kitchen and grabbed the envelope. She wasn't technically violating Greg's privacy since the envelope wasn't sealed.

When Farah opened the envelope she gasped! "Oh my God! Oh my God!" she yelled.

She paced back and forth across the room. Farah grabbed the remote, threw it across the room shattered a picture of Bryann and the dog, Talcum. Tears burst from her eyes.

She flipped through the pictures. There was shot after shot of her with Kane. Someone had been following them. There were shots of the apartment, the kiss on the pier, and even her naked breasts from the back seat of the car. Farah immediately grabbed her phone and called the girls.

Within minutes Liv came crashing through the front door. "What the hell?"

Farah could barely see Liv through her tears. She tossed the envelope to Liv who began her version of "Oh my God! Oh my God!" She looked at each picture with her eyes bulging from her head. "Holy hell, Farah. This is bad."

"I know." Farah stood in the middle of the room. She stared at her friend and her eyes said it too all.

Liv responded to Farah's silent plea. "I don't blame you honey. I'll fix us both one." Liv ran out the front door, just as Callie entered.

"What's going on?" Callie asked. "Where is she going?"

"To get me a drink," Farah said, still stunned. She looked at Callie without blinking.

"A drink! What's going on?"

Farah tossed her the envelope. Callie stared at each picture for what felt to Farah like a full five minutes. She slid one picture after the other to the back of the pile. "There has to be forty or fifty shots here," Callie said.

Callie put her arms around Farah and led her to the sofa. "Sit down. I'll get you some water. WATER!" She reiterated to her sober friend. "Don't fall down now Farah. It's been too long. We can deal with this together."

Farah curled up on the couch but said nothing. When Callie came back into the family room she sat next to Farah. "So, who do you think did this?"

"Greg," Farah whimpered. "He must have hired someone to follow me."

"Are you sure? Why would he do that?"

"Who else could it be? Who would have known I was going into the city today?"

Callie grimaced, "But why would he send himself and envelope? Maybe Kane is blackmailing you."

"Oh Callie, stop it! After all these months? He's had plenty of opportunity for that. Besides, he didn't know where we were going today. It was a total surprise to him."

"Are you sure?"

"Yes! Trust me. He didn't even like my surprise." Farah began to sob. "It's Greg. I know it."

"But you don't really know this guy, Farah."

Farah looked at Callie, "Will you please stop it! Kane had nothing to do with this. I've been with him everyday for almost a year."

"That's the problem," Callie interjected.

Farah rolled her eyes. "Just tell me what to do Detective Piper. Be my friend and tell me what to do."

Callie exhaled. "Okay, well the first thing we have to find out is who is behind these pictures. Then we go from there."

***

Kane couldn't help but think that one day he and Farah would be like his parents who had been married for over forty years and still enjoying each other's company. They sat across from him in the booth with their shoulders barely apart. They touched each other every few minutes. Still in love after all this time. He wanted that for himself and for Farah. She deserved to be happy.

His mother gave her best attempt at re-telling a joke she heard when the punch line was interrupted by the buzzing from Kane's phone. Dreadfully, he picked it up. "Hello."

"What's up? Where are you?" His cousin's voice caused him to groan on the inside.

"I'm out with mom and dad."

"Oh tell them I said hello."

"What do you want?" Kane asked. "I'm busy." Kane motioned to his parents that he needed to take the call and stepped away from the table.

"You sound chipper today. I guess sex in the back seat of a sedan will do that to you."

Kane could not take another step. He stood frozen without even a blink. "What did you say?"

"You heard me. You had a wonderful day in New York with your girlfriend. Didn't you? Walking hand in hand, kissing, grinding and moaning for anybody around to see. Yuck! Man, you are sprung."

"You saw me out today?" Kane mumbled.

His cousin gave a victorious sigh. "Not exactly. You were so until your girl that you didn't even notice the person following you taking pictures. Oh, and that shot of you on your knees at the car door. That looked like a proposal to me."

"You're having me followed?" Kane growled in anger.

"Yep. You can go ahead and be in love now because I got what I needed. Your debt is paid in full."

"Riley!" Kane shouted and the waiter shook his finger at him.

"Zo!" She mocked back at him then hung up the phone.

Kane trotted back to the table and excused himself from dinner. As soon as he got outside of the restaurant he dialed his phone.

"Hello?" Stormy was surprised to hear from her cousin. "Alonzo, what's up?"

"Nobody calls me that anymore." He was annoyed. "I need Kendall's number," Kane said.

"Uh-Oh, what did she do now?" Stormy asked. "I knew this was going to end badly."

"I need the number, Stormy. Now."

"Tell me what is going on. I know my cousin and maybe I can help without involving Kendall."

"No you can't help with this one. I really need that number, Stormy. Please." Kane's voice began to crack.

He wished he had never gotten involved in this whole mess. He should have known when Riley got him the job at the package company that she was up to something. She had set him up too and now it was his turn to be on the offensive.

"I've had enough of her. For years we all sat back and let her manipulate us in her schemes. No more."

"She really does mean well, Zo."

"Stop calling me that. My name is Kane!"

"No, Uncle Kane is "Kane" you are "Zo" or would you prefer we call you Junior?" Stormy laughed. "Anyway, tell me what she did this time."

"Just give me the number, Stormy."

"You know she's just..."

"...Evil?" Kane declared.

"No, not evil. Broken. She's been through a lot. And underneath that tough skin of hers she's hurting."

"I don't want to hear it. Are you going to give me the number not?"

"Okay, I'll text it to you when we get off of the phone," she said.

"I don't have text."

"What! What do you mean you don't have text? Everybody has text messaging."

"Not me I have regular phone."

"A rotary?" Stormy laughed.

"Give me Kendall's number," Kane groaned.

-10-

Liv came back to the house with two bottles of Vodka and cosmopolitan mix. "The goose is loose," she said as she slammed the bottles onto the coffee table.

"Liv, get that stuff out of here. Farah hasn't had a drink in ten years and she's not going to start back now." Callie grabbed the bottles from the table, but Farah grabbed them from her hand.

"I need a drink," Farah sighed. "One drink is not going to completely knock me off the wagon."

"Really?" Callie snipped. "And where is that in the AA manual?"

Liv pushed her hand towards Callie's face . "It's just after the 'what to do when your shit blows up' section of the book."

"Some friend you are Olive," Callie frowned.

"Honey, we aren't going to let you go back down that road again. One drink is not going to hurt you." Liv pulled a martini shaker from her bag, went into the kitchen and came back with ice and plastic cups. "I don't know why I thought you'd have martini glasses but these will do us fine."

Liv gave the girls a cup and poured a cold, freshly shaken cosmo into each one. She gave Callie a look. "Drink it!" she said in a stern tone.

Callie rolled her eyes and took a sip.

 Farah took her first drink in over ten years, closed her eyes, and remembered just how good a freshly chilled cosmo tasted. The cranberry and lime taste swirled around her taste buds like a prima ballerina. After that first drink, which she savored, Farah gulped the rest of the cup down like a shot and poured herself another. "You know, I don't care if Greg finds out about Kane."

"Yep, that's the alcohol talking already," Callie said. Liv agreed.

"No seriously, I know I want to be with Kane so why hide it."

"Farah," Callie took a sip as if preparing to deliver a speech. "You don't know anything about this guy except what he has told you about himself."

"Which is all most people know about the person in their life; not everyone has stellar detective skills and access to government databases." Liv added.

"Just let me do some digging before you throw everything away." Callie waited for Farah's response. "If nothing turns up I promise not to say another negative word. If you want to go down this road, I'll be here for you."

Farah stared out across the room. "Fine. But it won't matter what you find. I love him. He loves me. We want to be together in a relationship that we don't have to hide."

Callie shook her head, "Yeah, well for now let's focus on how to handle this stack of pictures with you and your 'lover'. I told you about having a lover. Isn't this exactly why we made the pact to hit it and quit it? This could be disastrous for your family, particularly for Bryann who is facing enough right now."

Farah knew Callie was right. Despite her love for Kane she needed to be strategic in how to handle this. "It is so odd because Kane just warned me today to be careful. He said we should not jeopardize our case with Bryann. He said we should wait until after the trial to be together."

"That was so sweet of him," Liv slurred.

Callie rolled her eyes. "Liv, you are such a hopeless Pollyanna," she continued. "OR perhaps he knew someone was about to happen. Did you call him?"

"Not yet." Farah took another gulp of her drink and let out a delighted moan.

"Why not?" Liv asked inside of a hiccup.

Callie smirked. "Because it crossed her mind that it could be him. Didn't it? You are as stupid in love as you claim to be? That's my girl!"

"Nope," she said and finished the last of her third plastic cup of high octane cosmopolitan. "I don't think it's him in my heart. But my mind keeps rehearsing all the things my Aunt Janice taught me over the years about men, particularly that kind of man."

"What kind of man?" Callie asked.

"Street men. Hood boys. You know..." Liv said.

"Typical Niggas," they all recited in unison.

"Yeah..." Farah sighed. "I hope my heart is right."

A few minutes later Bryann came in the door. She had a wry smile on her face when she walked into the room. She was most definitely high on something. She sniffed Farah's cup. "Mom! Are you drunk?"

"No! Well, maybe a little. Okay, yes," Farah stammered her answers out over a thick tongue.

"Cool!" Bryann laughed. "So can I drink with you guys?"

"No!" they all said in unison.

Bryann giggled. "It was worth a shot."

Liv poured about a quarter of the mix into a cup as if Farah wasn't sitting right next to her. "Here, and don't tell your mother."

Farah leaned her head back on the couch when the doorbell rang. "I'll get it," Bryann said as she jumped up.

"No!" the three said in harmony again. Callie stood quickly and nearly pushed Bryann out of the way. She went to the door with caution. Callie thought that it could be another blackmail package. She opened the door. "Can I help you?" She asked the beautiful woman who stood in the doorway.

It took only a few seconds before Callie realized that the woman looked just like Bryann. Same grey eyes and milky beige skin. "Liv!" she called out calmly and tried to cover her panic.

Liv got up from the sofa. "Now what? Can't I have a moment's peace from those damn boys? They are probably hungry or fighting," she sighed. "I'll be back," she told Farah.

When Liv turned the corner into the foyer she knew immediately why Callie had called her. She took three shaky steps toward the door. "Wow!" She examined the woman's face. "You must be Riley Briggs. You look just like Bryann."

"I am glad to see I'm well known," Riley said as she looked down at her fiery red nail polish as if bored. "Is Dr. Goodwyn home?"

"You need to leave her now," Callie warned. "Or I will arrest you for trespassing."

"Oh, you are the detective friend, Callista Piper." Riley extended her hand. "Nice to finally meet you."

"Hey," Liv hiccupped in a slur. "How do you know her name?"

"Oh! And you must be the drunken Olive Jones. Damn! You really do drink all day every day."

Callie interrupted. "Not sure where you got your information and don't care. You've got five seconds to turn around and walk away."

Riley put five fingers in the air and took one away slowly, one by one, as if she were counting down Callie's threat. When she got to the last two fingers her eyes popped open. Her expression made both Liv and Callie turn around. Bryann stood behind them. She was statue-like, stiff as a concrete board. Her eyes were locked on Riley.

"Who are you?" Bryann asked. Then she screamed. "Mommy!"

Farah sprung from the sofa because she knew something was wrong. If Bryann was calling for her "mommy" it meant trouble. When she took her first step she knew she was drunk. It was a long distance familiar feeling that rushed back to her. She stopped to gather her balance and took a deep breath. The room spun in a hazy blur.

When Farah came within view of the front doorway she didn't stop in shock like the others. As soon as she saw Riley's face, Farah sobered up completely. The mama bear came out of her like she always promised Bryann it would if there were ever trouble. Riley Briggs was trouble, big trouble.

Farah considered just rushing toward the door to tackle Riley. Then she took delight in the vision of herself slapping Riley to the ground. Her mind quickly went to burying Riley underground. Her jaws clenched so tight that there was strain in her neck.

"Mom, who is that?" Bryann asked.

Riley stood at the door for a moment more before she turned and quickly walked away. She had not intended for Bryann to see her. She only wanted to find out how Farah responded to the pictures. Riley left Greg's name on the envelope because she knew Farah would open it to see what was in it. But it just dawned on her that Bryann could have opened the envelope instead. She had not thought of that.

"Mom?" Bryann said again. "Mom!" She screamed. "Who was that?"

Callie stepped toward Bryann, "Honey, why are you so upset?"

"Aunt Callie, Stop! I want to know who that woman was? Tell me."

Liv leaned against the doorframe before she finally closed the door. She had not sobered up at all and so this whole ordeal made her head spin. "Bryann, sit down in the family room."

"Auntie Liv. Aunt Callie. I am not talking to you. I asked my mother who that woman was and I am not moving from this spot until she tells me." Bryann crossed her arms and scowled. She had picked up Greg's stubborn insistence when the occasion occurred to use it.

"Sweetie, let's talk when Dad gets home." Farah walked over to embrace her daughter.

"I knew it. He's having an affair with her isn't he?"

"What?" Farah, Liv, and Callie once again sang in harmony.

"No! What on earth would make you think such a thing?" Farah asked.

"I hear you guys fight over sex and you think I don't know that you aren't happy with dad. I know mom. I'm not a kid." Bryann unfolded her arms and stomped back into the family room like she used to do when she was a preschooler.

Farah smiled at Callie and Liv. Callie asked, "You want us to stay?"

Before Farah could answer the doorbell rang again.

Liv swung the door open. She started to yell before she could see who stood on the other side, "Look! You are not welcome here."

Much to Liv's chagrin, it was her mother-in-law. "Umm, okay, but the boys are hungry. I could fix them something to eat but I know you want them to eat all of that silly organic crap the chef brings. You know, I raised their father on good old fashioned American food and he turned out just fine."

Liv rolled her eyes. She said, "And the party is now over. See you girls later." Liv turned and walked out the door, closing it behind her.

Farah turned to Callie, "I need you to find out everything you can on that woman. Everything."

"What are you going to tell Bryann?" Callie asked.

"I don't know. I will think of something."

"The truth works." Callie said.

"Not today it doesn't." Farah crossed her arms the same way Bryann had just done. "Let me know what you find."

Farah took a deep breath and walked back into the family room where Bryann had managed to make herself a drink. Farah took the cup from her hand. "Young lady, I don't care how upset you may be, do not disrespect my home. You are not having an episode right now. You know full well what you are doing, don't you?"

Bryann put the cup down. She hung her head. "Yes."

Farah lifted her daughter's eyes to her own. "I made a mistake. I drank today and I should not have done that. Tomorrow, I'm back to being mom, who doesn't drink. Okay?"

Bryann nodded.

"You ready to talk?" Farah asked.

"Who was she?" Bryann's eyes watered.

Farah could not stand the pain that was building in her chest. Before she could even think about it, she said, "She's your father's mistress. You were right."

After the words flew from her lips, Farah knew she could not take them back. She also knew that she had just made the situation ten times worse. The end of this saga was going to be brutal and she knew it. She could only hope that Bryann would not hate her as much as she hated her Aunt Janice.

Bryann began to bawl with her head in her hands. Farah could not take it. "Baby, no she's not. I lied."

Bryann looked up at Farah with tears pouring down her face. She was yelling and crying at the same time. "Mom, what the hell is going on around here? Tell me who she was!"

"Well, sweetie, why is that so important to you? What are you feeling?"

"Don't freakin' try to psychoanalyze me!"

"I'm not, but I want to know why you had such a reaction to that woman?"

"What woman?" Greg's voice startled both Farah and Bryann. "Is that vodka?" Greg asked. He dropped his brief case on the floor and stood with a puzzled look.

"We didn't hear you come in honey," Farah said.

"I can see that." Greg still had not moved from his position. "Why are there four cups and two vodka bottles in my house when we don't drink."

"Greg, sit down."

"No, I'm going to stand until I get answer," he said. There was that stubborn insistence that Greg used to command his position.

Farah frowned, "Greg, please sit down." She repeated in a more harsh and agitated tone this time. Now was not the time for a power struggle.

He tilted his head to one side as if to say, "Did you hear me?" But he did not move.

Finally Farah blurted, "Riley Briggs came here today."

Greg immediately took a seat in the chair across from them.

"And Bryann thought that you were having an affair with her."

"What? Why would you think that sweetheart?"

"I don't know. It was the way everyone was looking at her." Bryann said. Her eyes were blood red and tears streamed down her face. "Auntie Liv and Aunt Callie were furious. So was mom."

Farah and Greg looked at each other. Greg said to Farah, "Are you drunk?"

"Not anymore," she answered.

Greg squeezed his forehead with both palms of his hands. "My wife is drunk. My daughter thinks I'm cheating. I have lost control of this family."

"Not really about you right now, honey." Farah said in tone that made Bryann smile. "Bryann was very emotion when she saw Ms. Briggs. I'm trying to figure out why."

"She told you why. She thought I was having an affair with her." Greg's words were a deliberate warning for Farah not to go any further. He was adamant about not telling Bryann about the adoption.

Farah gave Bryann an embrace and kiss on the cheek. "Sweetie, can you let Dad and I have a talk for a minute and then we can come upstairs and talk with you."

Bryann looked back and forth between her parents. "Sure."

On her way out of the room she bent down to grab a cup of drink but Farah grimaced and she put it down. Farah watched Bryann walked up the stairs. When she turned around Greg towered over her in front of the chair. His face was bright red and she noticed he was looking down at the floor beside the loveseat. Farah just dropped her head.

"What the..." Greg bent down to pick the photos.

Farah stayed silent. In all the commotion with Riley, she had completely forgotten that the envelope and pictures were still lying where she had tried to hide them from her daughter.

"Farah?" Greg questioned. "What's this?"

-11-

There was nothing that Farah could say about the pictures that would ease Greg's mind or her own. So she said nothing at all. She sat without taking her eyes off of him. He stood there waiting for her to say something that would explain the pile of photos.

"Who took these?" Greg asked.

"Don't you know?" Farah responded. As a psychiatrist she knew that answering a question with another question was strongly evasive and convincingly confessional.

"No, I don't. Why would I know who took these?" Another question from Greg made him look suspicious to Farah. "More importantly, who is this man in the picture?" Greg tapped the palm of his hand on his head the way they do in the "V-8" commercials. "Of course, this is why you've been so defensive of Black men all the sudden."

"What?" Farah rolled her eyes. "I haven't the slightest idea what you are talking about right now Greg."

"I'm talking about these pictures of my wife, riding the hell out of a Black man in the backseat of a car, like a teenager." He shook his head. "I would understand getting pictures of Bryann like this. But, what's so special about this guy that you just put it all out there. Why isn't he like the others?"

Farah's eyes widened. She swallowed. "The others?"

Greg let out a flow of forced air. It wasn't a sigh. It was more like he exhaled to prepare for what was next. "Yes, Farah. The others. The other four men that you have had sex with since we've been married. The Spanish guy at the medical convention in Chicago, the TV sports guy, that ridiculously metrosexual R&B singer and The Verizon guy..."

"You knew about that?" Farah was glad Greg knew of only a few of the men she had been with during their marriage. The truth was that she had been with many men. Hell, she had been with more than four Verizon guys in the last fifteen years. Greg's count was way off and Farah was relieved, but still shocked that he knew about any of it at all.

"Of course, I knew. I'm your husband. I've known you since you were nineteen years old. Greg stopped his monologue. "But who is this?" He pointed at the picture of Kane.

Farah was nearly in shock. Thankfully, Greg did not know of all of the men in her past. If he did, there would be no way he could stay married to her. No man could handle that level of betrayal from a woman and she knew it. Even if he loved her enough to stay, his ego would not allow it. Farah learned about Ego in the first year of medical school. It was Freud 101. Ego trumps all unless otherwise trained to be silent.

Farah took a deep breath. She curled her feet up under her on the sofa and grabbed a pillow. "His name is Kane Taylor. He's a guy I met at my office."

"A patient!"

"No. No." Farah scoffed. "He's the...the...the delivery guy."

"The delivery guy...as in courier service packages?" Greg asked.

Farah nodded. Somehow the way Greg said it made her feel embarrassed and ashamed. She had actually fallen in love with the guy that delivers her mail.

Greg sat down beside her. He moved the pillow from her lap and held her hands. "Farah, sweetheart. How does a beautiful, brilliant, educated, well-respected woman like you end up with the package delivery guy? Look at this tattoo on his forearm. Seriously.

"You have a tattoo Greg," Farah defended.

"Yeah not like that. That's a prison tattoo."

"No it's not. He did not get that until he got home." Farah was adamant before she realized how she sounded defending her lovers tattoo choice.

"I'm not the psychiatrist in the family. You are and you are an excellent doctor. I want you to ask yourself a question and figure out the answer. I don't need to know the answer, but you do." Greg paused. "Why are earth do you behave this way?"

Farah sat in silence. Finally a tear fell down her face. Then streams followed. She and Greg were eye to eye, holding hands. The look on his face said he needed answers. She still could not believe that he knew of her past indiscretions, yet never mentioned them. He never treated her any differently than the highly regarded wife that he promised she would be on their wedding day.

Finally, she spoke. "I love him, Greg."

Greg acted like he couldn't hear her. He did not blink, breath or blush. He just sat there waiting for a better response.

Farah dropped her head. "He makes me happy. I want to be happy."

Greg sat there for a few more seconds without a blink or a sigh. Then he exploded into a rage that Farah had never seen. "Are you out of your mind? We are in a battle for our daughter. The family that we...no I...have worked so hard to keep together is under attack and you decide you are in love with a package deliver guy. I have stayed with you despite all your sordid, misguided behavior and you can look at me in my face and tell me that you love a package deliver guy."

Greg walked to the other side of the room. He rustled his hand through his hair. "Aunt Janice was right. You are nuts like your mother." He picked up the photos and threw them all across the room. Then he kicked the chair so hard that he put a hole in the upholstery.

Farah bawled. "That's mean. You are trying to hurt me."

"And you aren't trying to hurt me Farah? What the hell is wrong with you? I get it. You like to have sex with men you aren't attached to so you can be yourself. I've read enough books about it to know that Aunt Janice messed you up with all the 'good girl vs bad girl' talk. You can't have good sex with me because you have some idea of what a wife should be in bed but this guy...the damn package deliver guy... gets sex in the South Street seaport parking lot."

"What do you want from me?!!!" Farah cried.

"I want sex in the freaking South Street Seaport parking lot and in the Barclays garage and on top of the car at the varsity baseball field. I want those things from my wife. She likes it. I like it. So why can't we like it together?"

Farah continued to cry. Bryann rushed back down the stairs. "What are you guys yelling about?"

"Go back upstairs," Greg yelled.

"Dad.."

"Go! We'll be up in a minute." Farah shouted to Bryann who immediately turned back and stomped up the stairs.

Greg paced back and forth across the room from the fireplace to the projection screen. Back and forth he walked and ran his hand through his hair before grabbing a handful into his clutches. Farah had cried more in the past ten minutes than in the past ten years of her life. She knew it was because Kane had opened her up to her feelings again. Before she met him she was a stoic, a very controlled, emotionally calculated being. Now, she was a human being. Not only was she human, but she was also a full-blown feeling, crying, loving emotional woman. All of her pain was pouring out her.

"I always knew you were a roller coaster rider forced into a carousel lifestyle. I knew it." Greg said in frustration.

"That's not true. I love our life."

"Do you Farah? Do you? So much that you can't go six months without having an affair."

"That's not..." Farah stopped. It was true. She had consistently cheated throughout their marriage. There was always something missing from them and she spent the early years trying to figure out what it was. Finally, she stopped trying to figure it out and just did what she could to fix it. Farah wanted passion. She found it in a lot of places. What she didn't realize is that she also wanted love and she found it with Kane.

"I'm not letting you leave," Greg said. "Not now. Not when we have this fight on our hands. Did you tell me that she was here today?"

"Yes," Farah sniffed. "She was."

"And she sent these pictures I guess."

"I don't know," Farah responded. "Callie is on that part."

"Well, if she did we are in trouble. We can't very well convince a judge that our family is so stable and functional that an outside presence would disrupt it." Greg growled. "We can't argue the well-being of our daughter when you are having sex in parking lots in broad daylight." Greg grabbed a few pictures and ripped them in half. "Damn it, Farah!"

The faint smell of marijuana floated down the stairs. Farah sniffed and then looked at Greg. "No she is not..."

Farah jumped up from the sofa and went upstairs. Greg followed. When they reached Bryann's room she was lying in her bed blowing smoke in the air. Farah went over and grabbed the joint from Bryann's hand. "Young lady, do not push me. You are out of line and you know it."

"And so are you guys!" Bryann screamed.

"Who are you yelling at?" Greg shouted.

"I will toss your little behind on this floor and slap you silly until you show us some respect," Farah yelled.

"Sure, Mom. Sure you will." Bryann said in laughter.

Farah turned and looked at Greg in disbelief. Her daughter had called her bluff and she knew it. Farah had never so much as laid a single finger on Bryann. She rarely even raised her voice at her daughter, but Farah's frustration was waging war on her composure and on that day she could have easily slapped the bipolar out of Bryann.

"You need to tread lightly little girl. I can't do this today." Farah said with folded arms. Farah mashed the joint out in the soda can that doubled as an ashtray. She stood for a moment and counted to ten in her head. It was time for her to pull it together because everything around her had spiraled out of control. "We need to talk."

"Well, I'm too tired to talk now." Bryann said and turned her back toward her parents.

Farah's head snapped around to Greg. "Now!" Farah screamed in a way that made Bryann jump up from the bed.

"Okay. Okay." Bryann rose up with a look of fear on her face. "Geesh, when did you turn into a Black mother?"

Farah's mouth flew open and a sort of indignant gasp flew out of her mouth. In that one moment she saw all the mistakes she had made with Bryann by being lenient with her. Greg had been right all along to punish Bryann for some of her antics, even when she wasn't on her meds. Farah always let Bryann's illness be the excuse for her bad behavior. Now

Farah could see that Bryann had learned to manipulate her. She never saw it before that moment.

"Go to our room and sit down," Greg ordered his daughter.

Bryann walked down the hall and Greg and Farah looked at one another trying to communicate without words. Farah's eyes said, "Should we tell her?" Greg's face, frowned into deep wrinkles, said, "This is all your fault."

They all entered the room. Before Farah could sit down beside Bryann, Greg blurted. "Your mother has something to tell you."

Farah looked at Bryann who appeared to be glassed over from both being high and confused from all the activity that had happened that day. "Your father did not have an affair. I did."

"You did?" Bryann's face contorted. "Yeah, right." She rolled her eyes.

"I did. And I'm very sorry for the pain I've caused your father."

"I don't believe you. You would never cheat on Dad. Please!" Bryann looked at Greg. "He would cheat on you though."

Greg flinched. "You are dead wrong. I have never cheated on your mother. Not one time. And I do get approached often. I love your mother."

Farah looked at him with a "yeah right" look. She knew Greg well enough to know that if he had knowledge of her past exploits he definitely vindicated himself with a little something of his own. Maybe not multiple times, but at least once.

"Sweetheart, your father and my problems are not your concern and I'm sorry that you have to even be privy to this information." Farah sighed. "The truth is people make mistakes."

"Not you. You never make mistakes." Bryann said.

"I just had vodka tonight after over ten years of sobriety. I make mistakes, Honey."

"Wait, so if all of this is about you cheating, who was that woman at the door?" Bryann asked. She looked at her father for answers.

He looked at Farah for direction. His eyes begged her not to tell but she had told enough lies for the day -- for a lifetime. Farah grabbed the sides of Bryann's face. Her daughter's eyes were blood red and glassy but Farah could see that Bryann was paying close attention. "The woman's name is Riley Briggs."

"Okay, who is she."

Farah looked back at Greg. It took the words nearly a minute to rise from her gut and out of her mouth. Tears streamed down Farah's face. Greg was only a shade from being plum colored. Farah could see Bryann's breath was quick and she started to cry as a reaction to her parents' angst.

Greg sat down beside Bryann and wrapped his arms around both of them. Farah laid her head on Bryann's shoulder. By that point, Bryann was no longer high but sobbing for a reason she did not understand. She waited for her parents to explain.

Farah whispered quietly, "Riley Briggs is your birth mother. You are adopted."

-12-

The buzzer interrupted Riley's thoughts. She felt that soon she and Kendall would be together. He had been such a good father to his daughter with Lorraine that she knew he would want Bryann to be apart of his life. Then, they could begin their life together.

Riley grabbed her wallet and walked to the door expecting to pay the pizza guy. When she opened the door, Kendall and Kane stood with angry looks on their faces. "Kendall!" she squealed and leaped into his arms. "I knew you would come."

He kissed her on the cheek then lowered her back to the ground. "Yes, I'm here and I am not happy." Kendall's deep baritone voice, even when scolding, made Riley tingle inside.

Riley glared at Kane. "What did you tell him?"

"The truth. Something you aren't familiar with these days." Kane said

Riley swung the door open for the men to enter. She turned her back to them and walked away. "Look if this is going to be a 'shame on you Riley' meeting you can save it." She sucked her teeth and rolled her eyes.

"It's not a shame on you Riley meeting," Kendall said and looked around the apartment. "Am I paying for this?"

"Yep." Riley flopped down on the sofa. "So feel free to make yourself at home."

Riley looked at Kendall and her eyes danced. His creamy mocha skin had not aged since the day she met him. He was still just as smooth as ever. A modern day Billy Dee Williams type, Kendall was the only man that ever rocked Riley's world. Their relationship started as a mentoring relationship. Kendall was one of the largest and the most successful real estate developers in the Midwest. He had major juice in Cleveland, Detroit, and Chicago. He built a real estate empire from what he called "The Gentrification Gap" - young urban professionals that wanted nice, safe, luxury neighborhoods but to remain in the city near the people and action.

Riley was one of the realtors that sold many of his properties. He saw her tenacity and smarts and decided to mentor her. It took very little time for Riley to seduce him into what has turned into over 15 years of laughter, pain, tears, drama, and loads of fun for her. He went from being her mentor to her lover. Though Riley was engaged to her ex-husband at the time, she made a move on Kendall without any regard for his wife. She wanted him and he wanted her just as badly. Their partnership was more than sexual. It was mental, financial, and in a misguided, ridiculously skewed way, they considered it spiritual.

"I found our baby, Kendall," Riley said with a smile.

"She's not OUR baby, Riley. We decided to give her up for adoption. She belongs to the Goodwyn's now. She's their daughter."

Riley looked at Kane, "So you told him everything. Your version, I presume."

"Farah doesn't deserve this. She's a wonderful person. I love her and I'm not going to let you destroy her family." Kane threw his car keys down on the glass coffee table and Riley arched her brow.

Riley shouted at Kane. "Oh, you want her to stay married? Bull! You want her family destroyed as much as I do."

"Yes...No. Of course not," Kane sighed, "You know what I mean. Not like this."

"So you are just going to be her side guy for life? Hmph! I didn't think you had that in you dear cousin." Riley scoffed. "That's a lot to put up with for love. Trust me. I know."

Kendall's deep voice triggered, "Well, we are all surprised at what we're willing to put up with from someone we love." He shook his head at Riley. "Baby, why are you doing this?"

"Because she's our daughter and she deserves to know us."

"This is so complicated. The girl is almost sixteen years old. Why mess up her life?" Kendall asked.

"It may be hard for a while, but eventually we will all settle in and your daughters can have a great relationship. They are sisters."

Kendall looked at Riley. "We are not involving my daughter in this mess," he said with a stern tone and sharp eyes.

"Mess?" Riley paused. "So my daughter is mess but Lorraine's is YOUR daughter."

"Damn it, Riley! Stop! Don't make this about you and Lorraine. Girl, I have been with you for almost twenty years. Don't question my love for you. You get more of my time and my money than my own wife does."

"And? Charge it to the game," Riley said. Her vulnerability was gone and she pulled from all the experiences she had gained from her mother and aunts, who were masters at manipulating men. "I want our daughter and you need to make it happen. So Lorraine is just going to have to get over herself and deal with the fact that I had your first child."

"It's not a competition," Kane said to Riley.

"Shut up! This is all your fault. You think you love your precious little doctor. She's just as scandalous as I am. She told me so herself."

"Unlike you, she doesn't lie. I know all about her other affairs. That was before me."

"Blood is supposed to be thicker than water." Riley said.

"Yeah, well just a few days ago you were willing to feed me to the uptown boys so I think I'll go with water this time." Kane's words were interrupted by his phone's vibration.

"For the love of God, get a new phone." Riley growled at Kane as he walked into the other room. She turned her focus back to Kendall and stretched out seductively on the couch. "Now did you come all this way not to give me a proper greeting?"

"Riley." He chuckled and shook his head.

She used her finger to signal him, "Come here Daddy."

Kendall chucked again. But like Riley knew he would, he came over to the sofa and kissed her. "I missed you," he said.

"Mmmm, I missed you too." Riley pushed out her bottom lip. "Honey, I just want someone to be with me. When you are with your family having big fun and laughs, I am all alone."

"Big fun and laughs? You know Lorraine hates me. We are only together for my daughter."

"How do I really know that?" Riley pouted with a little whimper. "What if you start loving her again?"

Kendall hated for Riley to be disappointed and mostly he hated when he was the one that caused her the disappointment. She kept her eyes locked on his face so that even when he turned away for a second, when he turned back she was right there. Her skills to influence Kendall had not diminished in all of these years.

"Help me get her back," Riley said. "Just go to court with me. Please."

Kendall thought for a moment. He knew even if he said no that Riley would end up pulling him into it. He had never been able to tell her no and actually mean it. He could not think of one time in almost twenty years that denied Riley anything she wanted. Maybe it was his guilt for being married. Maybe it was his love. Either way, he never wanted her to be unhappy.

Kendall sighed. "Okay. But promise me that you'll let me explain all this to Lorraine for myself."

"Deal," she said with a giggle. "I promise."

"Show me your hands," Kendall said.

Riley pulled crossed fingers from behind her head. "Just kidding," she said.

She opened her mouth and kissed Kendall so deeply that she felt it in her back and thighs. The kiss caused them both to moan at once. That's just how connected they were to each other.

Before they could take it any further, the kiss was interrupted by Kane who ran back into the room. "Bryann tried to kill herself."

"Brian? Who is he?" Kendall looked at Riley.

"Bryann is our daughter," Riley smiled at him.

"Did you hear what I said, Riley? She tried to kill herself!" Kane grabbed his keys from the coffee table.

"Where are you going?" she asked.

"I'm going to the hospital to be with Farah."

"Are you nuts?" Kendall said.

"She needs me. She said she wants me there."

Kane opened the door then turned back to Riley. "You know, if my daughter were in the hospital fighting for her life, I'd probably be on my way there too. I'd be hysterical."

Puzzled, Riley looked at him as if she didn't understand what he said.

Kane shook his head. "You don't love her. You have no connection to her at all." He slammed the door so hard that the mirror on the wall fell to the floor.

"Do you think we should go?" Riley asked Kendall.

"No," he said. "I think we should leave the family alone."

"But what about our daughter?" Riley pouted.

"Riley, if you want a baby, I will give you a baby. All you had to do was ask." He said with a kiss to her neck.

"Really?" Riley began to think of herself pregnant again with Kendall's child. She envisioned them in the kitchen together eating takeout and flying down the expressway with the top down while the little girl yelled "weeeeeeee" from the back seat.

"No!" Kendall lifted his head. "Riley, we can't have a baby."

"Damn it, Kendall. Don't play with me." Riley growled. "I want our daughter in our lives. She needs to know who we are and I will keep pushing until I get my moment with her." Riley sat up on the couch. "I'm going to the hospital."

"No you aren't," Kendall forced her back down into a lying position. "That's the last thing the girl needs right now. Let's wait to see what Kane says."

"Okay, but as soon as she gets out, I'm going to see her and..." The door buzzer interrupted her.

"Expecting someone?" Kendall asked suspiciously.

"Yes, the pizza guy -- who I will take in that back room and blow if you don't agree to do this with me. You know I'll do it."

"Riley!"

"Kendall!" She mocked and headed toward the door. When she opened the door the pizza "guy" was a woman. Kendall fell into laughter. Riley turned around with a coy smile. "You're lucky."

She paid for the pizza and closed the door. She laid the pizza box in front of him and stood in the center of the living room with her arms crossed. "Well?" she asked.

"Fine." He knew he would regret that word.

-13-

Farah and Greg sat patiently in the waiting room. Callie and Liv flanked Farah on both sides. Greg, with Adam, sat across from them. He glared at Farah with a mix of anger and disappointment on his face. Farah was overcome with guilt. She taught her patients that shame was a wasted emotion but she was very ashamed at the moment.

"This is your fault," Greg said.

"It's no one's fault," Callie snapped at Greg.

Farah's nose and eyes drained fluid down her face. She wiped her nose with the bottom of her tank top and looked down at her bare feet. When she heard Bryann scream out in horror, she didn't even take time to put shoes on her feet before throwing Bryann into the car and racing her to the Emergency Room.

People usually try suicide by slitting their wrists or making minor cuts all over their body. Bryann was not the "usual" bi-polar patient. Even when she was well controlled on her medication, she had a challenging attitude that often needed adjusting by her parents.

After hearing what Farah and Greg had to say, Bryann calmly walked down to the kitchen, grabbed the largest carving knife and rammed it into her stomach. She had been in surgery for hours already and the only thing they were told was that the doctor was doing her best.

"This never would have happened if Farah had not - " Greg asserted.

"Had not what, Greg?" Farah looked up at him. "If Farah had not what?"

"Never mind," Greg said.

"Bryann isn't lying in there fighting for her life because I had an affair. She's not gaping wide open on an operating table because I had a drink. She didn't hit bottom because we lied to her for her entire life. She tried to kill herself because that woman - Riley Briggs - came to my doorstep. And that's something she will regret for the rest of her life." Farah's voice shook as she spoke. "So if you want to blame someone. Blame her. Blame her for setting off this chain of events. Blame her for the genetics she passed down to my daughter. Blame her for being such an irresponsible excuse of a woman. Blame her!!!" Farah shouted.

"Shhhh," the attendant hushed.

"Don't you hush me," Farah snapped. The attendant looked away.

A few moments later the attendant walked over to the group. "Doctor Goodwyn?"

"What!" Farah snarled.

"Umm, there is someone to see you in the ER lobby. He says he's here for Bryann."

Farah put her head in her hands. "Bring him in."

Liv, Callie, and Greg all had puzzled looks on their faces. Farah avoided eye contact with them. At this point she needed comfort and the only person that could give it to her was Kane. She didn't care about Callie's judgment, Liv's excessive interest, or Greg's wrath. All she wanted was comfort.

When Kane entered the area he walked over to Greg first and extended his hand. "Hey, I'm sorry we had to meet like this."

Greg looked up at him with gritted teeth but remained silent. Adam grabbed Greg's arm, "C'mon man let's go for a walk." Adam looked down at Farah with such contempt that she burst into tears, but only for a brief moment.

Liv got up and walked with the guys so Kane could sit with Farah, who looked like she had been beaten with a stick at this point. Her mascara had run down her face leaving a double trail of black. Her eyes were puffy and her nose was red.

"Callie, you want to walk with us?" Liv asked.

"No," she said. Callie folded her arms and nestled into her seat. She gave Kane a look that could slice ice.

"Hi Callista," Kane said.

Callie flung her hand in the air - a very passive and begrudged hello.

"How are you doing baby?" Kane asked Farah.

"Ugh," Callie bellowed and got up from her seat. She followed behind Liv and the guys.

"Did you bring me some shoes?" Farah asked.

"Yeah." Kane reached in his duffle bag and pulled out a pair of sparkly flip-flops.

Farah gave him half of a smile, "Thanks."

She looked down at the shoes. They were the right size and she shook her head.

"What's wrong? Did I get the wrong size?"

"Nope. You got the right the size. You got a pair that I would wear anytime. You could have just picked up any old pair of flip-flops but you got these." Tears welled in Farah's eyes. "Greg has no idea what size shoe I wear. After all these years he still buys me a size 8."

"Baby, focus on Bryann, okay. Don't worry about anything else. Let's just give all our energy to Bryann."

Farah forced the corners of her mouth upward. Kane's presence made her feel safe. She did not feel any better and she wouldn't until Bryann came out of surgery. However, having Kane next to her gave her strength.

Farah began to cry again, "We should have told her long ago."

"You did what you thought was right at the time," Kane said.

"No I didn't. I did what Greg wanted me to do. I knew this would blow up one day. I just had no idea it would be like this. My baby..." she cried.

Kane wrapped his arms around her and she buried her head in his chest. The others came back into the waiting area. Liv sat beside Adam and held his hand while he sat with his other hand on Greg's back. No one spoke. No one acknowledged that Farah's lover had come from beneath the covers into everyone's present mind.

It was one thing for Greg to think Farah was cheating. It was something for the girls to know she was having an affair, but to see it with their own eyes was something different.

Callie, Liv, and Farah had many exploits along the way, but they never consorted together for any of it. Sure, they shared stories but they never involved the others in their relationships in order to preserve the collective friendship of the group. Now, it was out in the open and everyone sitting in that waiting area had to deal with it.

Liv pulled at flask from her purse, "I need a drink."

Callie snarled, "Oh God, Liv. Really?" She rubbed nudged Kane's arm out of the way and rubbed Farah's back.

"I'm okay," Farah said. "It's fine Liv. Go ahead. Have two shots for me."

Kane used a low voice to speak to Callie, "Has she been drinking?"

"I'm right next to you, Kane. I can hear you." Farah mumbled into her hands.

"Have you been drinking?" he asked in a disturbed tone.

"Yes, she has." Greg growled. "It's how all of this got started. She got drunk once she saw the pictures of you banging her on the seaport."

"Pictures?"

"Yes, someone took pictures of you and Farah while you were out this morning." Greg looked at Kane directly in the eye. "You wouldn't happen to know anything about that would you?"

"Uhh, no. No I don't." He swallowed and noticed that Callie watched him intently. "Who would do that?"

"We don't know," Callie said. "But I've got a team working on it."

Kane flashed an uncomfortable grin. "Oh good." He shrugged. His mind raced.

A few moments of silence passed when Greg asked Kane, "Do you know how many of you there have been?"

"None." Kane stated and his chest swelled.

"Ha!" Greg laughed. "Not quite. Your math is off. Don't you need to count the packages you deliver?"

"Look Dogg, I just came here to support Farah. I'm not here to cause trouble."

Farah sat quietly with her head down. She focused her energy on Bryann. At that moment she did not care if Greg and Kane broke out into a full blown brawl.

"Dogg?" Greg questioned. "Boy, address me with some respect."

"Boy? Who are you calling boy? You racist bastard." Kane stood up. So did Greg.

"Racist? Do you see my wife? Do you see my best friend? I'm not racist and you are a boy. You come in here wearing your t-shirt, saggy jeans and sneakers. You dress like a nineteen-year-old boy. Hell, you even have sex in cars like a teenager. Grown men take their ladies to hotels, nice ones. Ask Farah, she knows."

Farah was nearly catatonic. She heard everything that was said but did not bother to respond.

Adam spoke up, "You know, you brothers always want to cry foul when somebody speaks the truth to you. You are sleeping with this man's wife and the worst he called you was 'boy'. I'd have called you a nigga myself."

"Adam!" Greg was stunned. He had never heard Adam say that world. It was an agreement they made when they were seven years old. Greg would never say it or allow anyone else to say it - whether they were white or black.

Liv opened her flask and took a long gulp. "Dear Lord, you got my husband saying the n-word. In twelve years of married and three years of dating I've never heard him utter that word." She took another quick shot.

Greg and Kane stood facing one another with about three feet of "space and opportunity" between them. Callie stepped in the middle. "Gentlemen, let me remind you that this is a hospital and I am an officer of the law." She looked at Kane, "That's five-oh, po-po or whatever to you, hood boy."

Greg and Adam both chuckled.

"And you..." Callie continued. "Sit down and focus on your daughter, tough guy. What? Do you hold the championship belt in heavyweight money counting? Please!"

Adam laughed again. Callie glared at him and he stopped mid laughter. He didn't want to know what kind of witty remark she could come up with for him.

From around the corner, the doctor entered the room. "Farah?" she said. They were friends and had been since residency. Farah looked up at her. The doctor addressed the group. "We did the best we could do. We had to take out some of her stomach and liver. Thank goodness she missed her kidneys and we repaired her intestine wall."

Farah's raised her eyes toward her doctor friend with a questioning look.

"It's going to take months for her to fully recover, but we think she'll make it just fine. Physically, we've handled the problem. Psychologically, Bryann is going to need a lot of help. I don't know what brought this on but I hope it gets resolved for everyone's sake. She cannot endure another "accident" like this."

The doctor went on to explain the recovery process and that Bryann would be in the hospital for quite a while. Then she looked over at Kane. "I'm sorry, I don't believe we've met. I'm Dr. Shay Reynolds. I was a resident with Dr. Goodwyn and you are?"

"Uh," Kane froze. The group stared at him in anticipation. "I'm...I'm Kane Taylor. I'm Bryann's cousin."

Kane saw Greg's shoulders relax. This was one time where telling the truth actually got him out of trouble but would surely lead to more trouble very soon. He was indeed Bryann's second cousin and when Farah found out she would be devastated. He knew it. He had to find a way to remove himself from Riley's actions.

-14-

Farah spent most of her nights at the hospital with Bryann. She had stopped seeing patients in the office and the rest of her patient load was in the psych wing where her daughter was now recovering.

"Mom, when can I go home?" Bryann asked.

"It's going to be awhile, sweetie."

"But why? I'm fine. I just had a moment," Bryann whined.

"Baby, people don't have 'moments' like that one. Yes, everyone has down days and everyone may have a brief lapse of judgment. But, you took a knife and nearly gutted yourself. There is a problem and we have to get it fixed."

"But I'm on my meds."

"Medication doesn't fix everything. That's why I do what I do. We've depended on the medication to keep you balanced but you need therapy, regular therapy."

"Can't you do it?"

"No," Farah said. "I want someone that is in no way connected to me. I want you to have a completely unbiased experience."

Greg entered the hospital room, "That's a great idea."

Farah shot him a welcoming smile.

"Hi Honey." He said with a kiss to Bryann's forehead. "Farah, can I talk to you a minute outside?"

"Sure." She turned to Bryann with a kiss. "Be right back."

Farah and Greg went into the hallway. She saw his large duffle bag sitting beside the door and rolled her eyes. He looked at her and said, "I'm leaving."

"And you needed to bring the bag in for me to see it?" Farah scoffed. "Greg, this is no time for games. We need a plan to rehab our daughter - to rehab our family."

"I need to get away," Greg said.

"Now?"

"Yes, now."

"But what about Bryann?"

"She'll be fine. I'll see her everyday, but I can't stand the sight of you any longer."

Farah was half shocked and half relieved. "We have to be in court tomorrow. We can't tell the judge that we are separated. It will really complicate things."

"Farah, Bryann tried to kill herself. She's been in the psych ward for weeks. There is no reason to pretend that we have the perfect family. I say we just let the woman see Bryann."

"What? No." Farah whispered because she was cognizant that Bryann may be listening.

"For once let's just be real with ourselves," Greg whispered. "I'm tired of pretending that you love me. I'm tired of pretending that we conceived Bryann. I'm just tired of pretending."

Farah's heart jumped. She had been waiting to hear those words from Greg for many years. She always felt like their life together was some kind of movie role. He was the doting and providing husband. She was the beautiful, smart, well-respected wife. Neither of them ever stepped out of their roles to assess the reality of who they actually were.

"I do love you, Greg." Farah grabbed his hand. "But I am not in love with you."

"I know that. And in order for us to move on as friends I have to leave or else I'm going to resent you. I already do." Greg sighed. "When I saw how you were with him, I knew you had changed. He is not some fling or secret crush."

"No he's not," Farah said and dropped her head.

"You love each other. You were willing to let him into the most intimate and critical part of our life...our family."

"But Greg..." Farah stopped herself. There was nothing more to say. Greg was right. Everything he said was true. Even though she knew it, it was still hard to hear.

"I realized it that day in the hospital. When the most precious thing in the world to you was in jeopardy, you wanted him to console you. Not me, your husband. You wanted him to comfort you when my daughter was in crisis. That says a lot."

Greg peeked his head back into the doorway. "Bye-Bye baby girl. I'll be back in a few hours to see you."

"Bye Dad." Bryann smiled and this time the smile actually shone through her eyes.

She was definitely getting better. But with all of the confusion that lie ahead, Farah wondered how long Bryann could maintain. As much as she wanted to bring her daughter home, Farah thought that keeping Bryann in the hospital until things got sorted out was a good idea. When Bryann came back home there needed to be no ambiguity. She needed a solid life with a solid plan.

Farah came back in to sit with Bryann. "I'll admit you look better," Farah said with a smile.

"I feel better, Mom. I'm telling you. I'm ready to go home." Bryann said.

Farah gave a warm half-smile with her eyes, "Not just yet, but it won't be much longer. Let's get you lined up with a therapist and make sure your meds are stable."

***

On the way home from the hospital Farah called Kane. She loved the way he answered the phone when she called. It was like he rehearsed before he picked up the phone. It was a very sexy and stony masculine "Hah-lo".

"Greg's leaving," she said.

"What happened?" Kane asked. He had a habit of asking what happened if he did not hear what was said. He really meant "say it again". It was a bizarre trait but Farah was tickled by it, along with everything else about Kane.

"Greg's leaving."

"Leaving to go where?" Kane asked.

"Leaving me. He said he sees how we love each other and he has to go. He said that there is no need for us to pretend anymore."

"W-w-wow!" Kane stuttered.

"I know," Farah said. "He also said that he thinks we should allow Riley Briggs to have visitation with Bryann."

"Whaaaaaa..." Kane said. "Oh that's not a good idea."

"I know, but I feel like I may not have a choice. Now that Bryann knows she's adopted she is going to have questions that need to be answered. Besides, I'm just ready for this whole thing to be over so we can get on with our life together. In all the turmoil, I still love you so much."

"I love you too, baby." He paused. "Can I come see you?"

"Where?" Farah questioned.

"Ummm, I don't know, but I want to see you. Right now."

Farah felt a pang in her stomach. Things had changed and so she had to take a deep breath and embrace it. "Why don't you come by my house," she said.

"Uh, okay. Are you sure?" Kane asked with excitement in his voice.

"Yes."

***

By the time Farah got to her house, Kane was parked in the driveway. He stepped out of the car and she saw he had new sneakers. Greg kind of had a point about Kane's choice of outfits. He always wore sneakers. Farah was kind of getting tired of seeing them. They were all high-end, nice-looking sneakers but she wanted to see him in something besides sneakers and his work boots.

Kane had a nice body and would look great in a tailored suit and great pair of slip-in loafers. She made a mental note to buy him some suits and shoes. If they were going to really be together then it was time for Farah to start polishing Kane.

When they entered the house Kane looked around. "This house is amazing."

"Thanks, we built it."

"So this is where it all happens." Kane had an uncomfortable look on his face. His mind visualized a happy family living in the house. "All the joy. All the fun."

When Farah saw his face she led him by the hand into the kitchen. She pulled a small bottle of vodka from beneath the sink cabinet. "You want a drink?" she asked.

"No. And neither do you," Kane said with a frown. "What's going on with you?"

"Nothing, there's a little left so I might as well get rid of it."

Kane grabbed the bottle and poured it in the sink. "There you go. Problem solved."

"Kane!" Farah was annoyed. "I can make my own decisions. One drink isn't going to hurt me."

"You already had one drink today right?" His face was so expressive. His eyes bulged. His forehead wrinkled and his mouth was open just a bit in an expectant pose.

Farah rolled her eyes. She was unsure how he knew about her earlier drink. She had poured a bit of rum in her coffee that morning. She thought of lying to him but then decided that would be a step backward in her sobriety. "Fine," she said. One side of her mouth turned upward into a coy grin. "Well, then come over here and intoxicate me."

Kane strolled over to Farah and lifted her up on the kitchen island. She pressed her lips against his and moved with intense friction. Her tongue explored his mouth and then moved up his neck to his ear. "Make the pain go away," she whispered.

Kane began undressing her. Farah had lived in her "dream house" over a decade and never had sex in the kitchen. It was a fantasy she long wished for and it was about to happen. He rubbed her thighs. When he squeezed her calves with gentle force, Farah let out a tiny gasp for air. Her spot.

He unbuttoned his jeans and pulled them to the floor. Then he got down on his knees and explored between her thighs with what he called "fifty kisses." It was his way of making her so hot and thirsty that she was nearly ready to climax by the time he entered her. Farah was full of electricity from her shoulders to her ankles. Every touch increased her anticipation of Kane forcing his body into hers.

Before he stood to his feet, he slyly pulled the condom out of his pocket. Kiss. Kiss. Tear. Kiss. Kiss. Slide. He stood in a commanding position and pulled Farah across the counter.

Their foreheads were pressed against each other. He gently wiggled his way into her opening and then...thrust.

Once he pushed past her barrier, physical and emotional, a deep breathy "Ouh" escaped from Farah. She felt it every time he entered her. It was a thrust toward her destiny. She felt whole with Kane inside of her. In the hundreds of times she had had intercourse in her life, never did she feel like "one body" until Kane entered her.

She wrapped her legs around his waist and he held her tight. He lifted her without allowing his body to escape hers. Slowly, he lowered both of them to the floor. The cold tile on Farah's back was barely noticeable - though she did have a moment where she got distracted by the dust along the kitchen island floorboard. She made a mental note to sweep under there in the morning. Then she quickly returned to the present moment.

Kane pressed his face next to hers as she grabbed the back of his head. She whimpered in his ear again, "Make it stop hurting Kane. Take away my pain."

-15-

They next day Farah and the girls arrived in court. Greg and Adam waited for them outside of the courtroom. Greg's iPad was on his lap as he read. His iPhone peaked from out of his jacket pocket. The blaring noise from his headphones was easily identifiable as the 1980's Beastie Boys. Farah could see that he was in battle mode. She was glad.

"Why are you walking like that?" Liv asked Farah.

"Girl..." was all Farah could muster.

"Does your back hurt or something?"

"Yes. I slept on the kitchen floor last night." Farah said with a grin.

Callie and Liv looked at her. "You didn't." Callie said sternly.

"She did," Liv answered for Farah.

"I did." Farah shrugged. "He's amazing. I am actually in love for the first time in my life. Real love."

"That's great." Liv squeezed an arm around Farah's shoulders.

"I hope you know what you're doing," Callie added.

"Callie, maybe you should open your heart to love again," Farah said.

"Love weakens you," Callie said. "Look at you. You can barely think straight."

"That's not true. My love for Kane has given me perfect clarity on what I want to accomplish in my life. His love pushed me to happiness, not weakness. Even Greg saw it. He said he's never seen me more affectionate and vulnerable than when I was with Kane."

"Like I said, I hope you know what you're doing," Callie asserted.

Greg and Farah spoke briefly with their attorney. He told them what to expect. He had seen the photographs and knew how damaging they could be. "A picture is worth a thousand words," the attorney told them, "but Bryann has the last word."

"The hospital staff is on their way," Farah said just as Bryann entered the building in a lovely navy blue suit and pearls that Farah had purchased for her earlier in the week. She looked like a young woman in control, even though two men dressed in all white flanked her. "She looks great. Doesn't she?" Farah asked Greg.

He gave no response.

Farah and Greg each kissed Bryann on opposite cheeks. Liv and Callie gave her a big hug. "I miss you guys," Bryann said. "When can I come home?"

"I'm not sure honey. We need to ..."

"Today." Greg barked and interrupted Farah's explanation. "You can come home today."

Farah looked at him. Without making eye contact with Farah, he grabbed Bryann's hand. The men in white followed behind like secret service.

Farah felt good about the attorney's assessment. He explained that even if the marriage was in trouble, as long as the child was not in danger the pictures should not matter. In fact, having the marriage in a shambles may possibly help. With the trauma that Bryann could sustain from the disruption, the judge may even wish to limit the change in her life - especially with her psychological condition.

Farah saw Riley's attorney look back at the courtroom door over and over again. "Maybe she won't show up," she whispered to Greg who had yet to say anything directly to her.

Whenever he spoke, he looked at their attorney. When she asked Greg a question he either did not answer or answered to their attorney. She was used to this kind of behavior from him when he was upset. Greg was keen on ignoring things that did not fit into his personal sandbox. As if ignoring them made them disappear.

Just moments before the judge came from chambers, Riley entered through the courtroom doors. Her navy blue, pinstriped suit was beyond form fitting. It was tight across her hips and thighs. The jacket was snug beyond a tailor's efforts. And of course, her breasts were pushed up out of the top of a

V-neck cotton shirt. Riley looked phenomenal, as usual but she was completely inappropriate for court.

Callie leaned forward over the divider and whispered in Farah's ear, "So that's who buys suits from Victoria's Secret. I always wondered who bought those."

Farah gave an awkward smile through quivering lips. "Bryann looks exactly like her."

"But you are her mother," Callie whispered.

"And you're a damn good mother, Farah." Liv leaned in with a wink of confidence.

Riley was the first person to testify. She explained her mindset and circumstance when she gave Bryann up for adoption. Farah got worried when she saw the judge nodding at Riley's confession, but her attorney warned her to show no emotion - good or bad.

Riley sounded pure and authentic through her entire testimony until a tall, broad, brown skin man entered the courtroom. He walked in hand-in-hand with a woman of small stature who was dressed in ivory with pearls. From that moment, Riley was rattled.

"Can you tell us why you request visitation now?" her attorney asked.

"Um..." Riley stammered unable to take her eyes off the couple in the back of the courtroom. "Uh..." She got quiet.

"Ms. Briggs?" he asked.

"Because she's my damn daughter!" Riley shouted. Her attorney's eyes bulged. "Look at her! Look at her!" Riley pointed to Bryann who sat quietly with her "body guards". "She looks exactly like me. I have rights to my own fucking child!!!!! You don't know this woman. She's not a good mother. She's just a ..."

"Objection!" Farah's attorney shouted.

"Sustained," the judge commanded. "Ms. Briggs. That's enough."

Riley's attorney grimaced. "No further questions, Your Honor."

When Farah's attorney declined to cross-examine, her mouth flew open. Greg slowly and calmly lifted his hand to silence her. He looked at her with a nod to let her know it was the right move.

Farah's shoulders relaxed. Greg was now interacting with her and it looked as if they were winning. Whoever the couple was in the back of the courtroom had completely flustered Riley. She turned around and yelled to the man. "You will regret this!"

The woman in pearls smiled graciously in response. Callie, the good detective, leaned forward and whispered something to Farah's attorney. He nodded and waited a moment before scribbling something on a pad. He slid the paper across the table far enough for both Farah and Greg to read. It read, "Father?"

Riley's attorney declared, "Your Honor, we have no further witnesses but request the right to call a rebuttal witness if necessary."

The day continued on with droves of witnesses coming to testify on the Goodwyn's behalf. One by one they entered the witness stand to talk about what wonderful parents Farah and Greg were to Bryann. More importantly each of them spoke about what wonderful people Farah and Greg were.

The last person to call was Callie. At that point, the attorney felt like there was no reason to put Bryann on the stand to state her wishes. Callie should seal the deal. She raised her right hand and boldly stated her name, "Detective Callista Piper."

"Detective Piper, how long have you known Dr. Goodwyn?"

"Over thirty years." Callie responded with a big smile toward Farah and Greg who were now holding hands in alliance.

Her testimony continued and showed the good nature of Farah, just as Adam's testimony had shown the good nature of Greg. Farah's attorney was pleased with Callie's testimony because he kept nodding and smiling at her answers. Finally after several more questions he said, "That's all."

Then came the cross-examination. That is when it got sticky. Riley's attorney had a nearly menacing but sarcastic grin draped across his face. "Miss Piper..."

"Detective." Callie corrected him.

"Detective Piper. You say you've known Dr. Goodwyn since childhood. Would you say she's made some poor choices during that time?"

Callie frowned the way she does when someone asks a silly question. "Yeah. Haven't we all? Isn't that why we are here today? Ms. Briggs' poor choice that she now regrets."

Greg squeezed Farah's hand and she tried not to smile at Callie's answer. She was good and Riley's attorney was not going to get anything out of her that she didn't want to give. Callie gave straight, honest answers without compromising Farah's trust or ability to mother.

In frustration, the attorney dismissed Callie from the stand. Both Farah and Greg felt good about the outcome. Their attorney scribbled a check mark down on the pad. He was pleased too. Then Riley's attorney cleared his throat. He looked back at Riley and she said, "Yes!" The judge scolded her outburst.

Farah prepared for the introduction of the pictures. She braced herself.

"Your Honor," the attorney stated. "We'd like to call rebuttal witness Kane Taylor to the stand."

Farah gasped. Her eyes filled with water. She leaned over to Greg, but he held a hand out to keep her from reacting. His jaw was clenched and Farah could see his neck turning nearly burgundy with rage. Their attorney wrote on the paper "WTF?"

Greg didn't react to his scribble so he leaned over and asked Greg, "How did she get a hold of him?"

Greg gave his best toothy smile, "I have no idea."

Riley watched them closely with a wide grin stretched across her face.

Kane entered the courtroom in a suit that he had clearly borrowed from someone. The jacket was too broad across the shoulders. The pants needed to be hemmed at least two inches. Farah's heart beat like a bass drum. Kane took the stand. He looked at Farah and Greg with sad eyes. He swallowed before stating his name. "Kane Taylor."

The Goodwyn's attorney stood to his feet. "Your Honor, I object. This man was not on the witness list."

"Rebuttal witness," Riley's attorney claimed. "We call him to refute the previous testimony as to Dr. Goodwyn's good nature."

"Overruled," the judge stated.

"We respectfully request a recess," the attorney shouted.

"I'm going to deny that request for now," the judge said and Farah's attorney sat in defeat.

"Mr. Taylor, Can you tell us how you relate to this case?" The attorney asked.

Farah braced herself for the response. She hoped he didn't choose the words "lover" or "mistress" or "boyfriend" or any other term that would shift the judges opinion of her.

Kane remained silent. He stared at Farah and she looked back at him. He saw that her eyes were dark and sad. This was the moment he had feared since the day he fell in love with Farah. He wanted to grab her and hold her. He could see that she was almost about to break. When he looked at Riley, she gave him an evil-eyed glare.

"Mr. Taylor, could you please answer the question," the attorney asked.

"I..I.." He paused and looked toward Greg and Farah, "I'm sorry."

Farah bursts into tears. She could not hold it any longer. Greg let go of her hand and did nothing to console her. His whole face had turned the color of a plum.

"Answer the question, Mr. Taylor," the judge instructed.

"I am the plaintiff's cousin." Kane dropped his head.

A collective "WHAT!" rang from the courtroom. Farah, Greg, Callie, Adam, and Liv all shouted at once and continued to murmur. Farah stood to her feet. Her mouth dropped open and her eyes poured with tears. She shook her head from side to side. A look of utter confusion masked her face.

Then Bryann, who was clearly bored with the entire process, said aloud, "What's the big deal about that?"

The judge slammed her gavel. "Order!"

Riley's attorney continued, "And how else do you play a role in this case?"

"The defendant, Farah Goodwyn, is my lover," Kane continued.

"MOM!" Bryann jumped from her seat and the men in white pulled her back down. "Get your damn hands off of me!" She pushed one of the men back down in his seat.

Riley smiled at the feisty nature of Bryann. It seemed that she didn't just look like her. She acted like her too. When Bryann pushed into the aisle and walked towards her parents, Riley stood to her feet. Bryann looked at her and posed something close to a warning growl. Riley sat back down. She was well aware of that kind of rage. Bryann reminded Riley of herself.

The Goodwyn's attorney stood to his feet. "Your Honor," he said in an exasperated sigh. "Might we now please have a recess?"

The judge allowed thirty minutes for everyone to calm down and recollect. "When I come back into this courtroom I want order and I want to get the bottom of how on earth this has come to pass in this way." She looked at Riley's attorney. "I want to see you in chambers."

The bailiff escorted Kane to a seat in the courtroom. He sat alone. Riley sat alone. Farah sat with her face in her hands. Crying uncontrollably while Liv and Callie tried to comfort her. Adam flanked Greg to make sure he didn't attack Kane. Finally, Greg took Bryann out of the courtroom to talk to her. When the men in white followed he shouted, "Just my daughter."

The couple that sat in the back of the room had begun an intense conversation. The woman was expressively speaking to the man and the man sheepishly made an effort to explain something. She stood to her feet and shouted, "You are a witch, Riley Briggs. You're an evil, treacherous, family destroying witch. You work for the devil himself."

The bailiff walked over and asked the man to calm his wife. Emotions ran high in the room and there was no need for anyone to go to jail. However, if the current behavior continued, they would all end up locked in a cell.

"Yes, she does." Kane mumbled, but in a loud voice without raising his head.

Farah lifted her face at the sound of Kane's voice, "And so do you! How could you do this to me? Cousin? Cousin? You set me up. All of this was just an act. You are going to regret this, Kane Taylor." Before she could go any further, Callie pulled Farah out of the courtroom.

-16-

The thirty-minute recess seemed like hours to Kane. He kept his head down and tried not to look at anyone. He was afraid that she would never forgive him, but he had to figure out a way to make this up to Farah.

Kane felt a hand on his shoulder. When he looked up Kendall was standing over him. Kendall sat down beside him. "Look man, just do the right thing. You know what the right thing is to do. Don't let Riley drag you down this path. Trust me...I know."

Kane laughed, "Yeah, I guess you do."

"So you really love that lady. Don't you?"

"Yup," Kane nodded. "I never thought it would happen like this."

"Oh, c'mon man. You knew this was going to get ugly. I mean, when your cousin gets involved, it is going to get ugly." Kendall chuckled. "It's just her way."

"No, I mean, I never thought that when I eventually found a woman to love she would be married. What part of the damn game is this?" Kane looked up at the ceiling of the courtroom.

Kendall's laugh was a deep bellow and it was hearty like Santa Claus. "Man, listen...you are preaching to the choir. When I married that woman back there..." he pointed to his wife, Lorraine. "I never intended to hurt her one day of her life. I'm not a cheater, man. I'm not a bad guy. I fell in love with Riley despite all my attempts to try not to. I can't stay away from that woman. I love her with every breath I take." Kendall paused. "And you think I wanted this shit?"

Kane smiled at him. "Point taken."

"No homo right here but I'm going to keep it real with you. And if you ever tell anyone I said this, I'll bust you in your mouth on sight. Got it?" Kendall frowned.

Kane nodded with a smile. He felt better already.

"Alright..." Kendall let out a deep breath, "Love is like a butterfly. You can't catch a butterfly by chasing it. It will fly away and elude you every time. BUT...when you are standing still, minding your own damn business...that sucker will come land right on your shoulder. You don't control who you love."

"That's deep," Kane said. "And yeah...no homo." They laughed.

"You can control who you live with, who you have kids with and who you marry. But you CANNOT control who you fall in love with. That's why the song says if you can't be with the one you love, love the one you're with man."

"Well, I'm by myself," Kane said.

"Then...no homo again...love yourself man. Love yourself. Do the right thing for this family." Kendall put his large hand on Kane's shoulder again and made direct eye contact with him.

"But don't you want to be with your daughter?" Kane asked.

Kendall grimaced, "Of course, when I saw her walk into this courtroom my heart stopped. She looks just like Riley

- the love of my heart. But Lorraine is my life and the Goodwyn's are her life. I don't want to disrupt that."

"On either side huh?" Kane frowned a bit.

"Man, don't judge me. There is no rulebook to this mess. I have talked to Lorraine and if the judge grants visitation then we plan to embrace the girl. But as of now, no one knows I am the father except Riley, me and you."

Kane nodded just as Farah came back into the courtroom. She did not make eye contact with him but moved quickly to her seat. Callie frowned at him and shook her head. Liv, who looked to be nicely buzzed mouthed to him, "Bastard!" but only spit flew from her mouth, no sounds.

When the attorney called Kane back to the stand he was ready.

"Restate your name for the record."

"Kane Taylor," he responded.

"And for the record again, how are you related to this case."

He looked at Farah with apologetic eyes. She glared back with unforgiveness. "I'm the plaintiff's cousin and I am in love with Dr. Goodwyn."

A gasp jumped across the courtroom. "Order," the judge shouted. She looked at Kane, "Proceed."

Riley's attorney stood tall in front of Kane. "And you met Dr. Goodwyn in her office, correct?"

"Objection!" Farah's attorney shouted. "Leading the witness."

"Sustained. Ask the question appropriately counselor." The judge instructed.

"Okay, HOW and WHERE did you meet Dr. Goodwyn?"

Kane smiled. He looked at the attorney right in his eye and said. "Riley hired me to seduce her."

"What!" Liv shouted before Adam could hush her.

Kane continued, "My cousin came to me over a year ago and asked me to find her daughter. I didn't know at the time that she knew exactly where her daughter was. She pulled some strings to get me a job delivering packages and she made sure I had Dr. Goodwyn's office on my route."

Tears streamed down Farah's face. Greg looked like he wanted to vomit. But Kane continued his testimony. "My cousin came up with a plan to break up the Goodwyn's marriage. She thought that if they were not a couple then she would have a better chance at getting her daughter back. No. Not back because she only wants to visit her. She doesn't want to raise her."

"Shut up!" Riley shouted and the judge slammed the gavel again. "Ms. Briggs, one more outburst and we'll be having a different discussion other than visitation."

Riley nodded. If she could shoot knives from her eyes she would slice Kane to pieces. He sat with confidence on the witness stand and told his truth. "I didn't want to do it at first, but Riley offered to help me with something..."

"And what was that?" The attorney was exasperated.

"She paid off my debt to some bad people."

"I see. Isn't it true that she paid off this debt in exchange for you helping to find her daughter. And when you found her daughter you became infatuated with Dr. Goodwyn and acted purely on your own. Ms. Briggs never told you to engage with Dr. Goodwyn. Only to find her."

"That is absolutely NOT TRUE," Kane said sternly.

"Oh, so explain to us how you were paid to fall in love with Dr. Goodwyn?" The attorney's tone mocked Kane and he became agitated.

"She didn't pay me to fall in love with Farah. She paid me to break up their marriage. But instead, I realized that Farah was a special woman and a wonderful mother..."

"...who cheats on her husband." The attorney finished.

"Who loves her family," Kane declared.

Kane saw Greg nudge his attorney to do something, but the attorney shook his head. The way things were shaping up there was no need for objection. Kane was doing an excellent job as a character witness.

Kane continued, "She refused my advances for months and then one day after I pushed so hard -- and held her iPad hostage--she caved."

Kane saw a little smile creep through Farah's tears. "I followed her to the coffee shop, where Riley and I had been tracking her travels for months. We knew what days and times she went to get her coffee. I arranged to meet her there."

Kane's testimony went on for a bit longer before the attorney decided to stop asking him questions. Before he left the stand, Kane looked up at the judge and said, "I know both of these women, Your Honor. There is no question who should have the influence of shaping a young person's life. Farah is a great mother."

After that, the Goodwyn's attorney declined cross-examination and then the judge made an interesting choice. She wanted to speak to Bryann. Flanked by her parents, Bryann agreed to take the stand. At this point there was not a dry eye in the courtroom. Even the strangers who just hang around the courthouse to be nosy had tears flowing. There was so much confusion and so much deceit. There was so much complexity.

"State your name."

"Bryann Goodwyn...I guess."

"Yes, that's your name," Greg said aloud and the judge frowned at him. He shrugged.

"Do you have anything you would like to say before I ask you a few questions," the judge said.

Bryann paused. "Yes...Yes I do. First of all, everyone keeps referring to me as 'the child'. I am not a child. I am a young woman. I'll be fifteen and I know my rights. I have the right to choose whom I spend my time with and whom I do not. This court cannot force me to visit that woman." She pointed at Riley. "Nor can this court stop me from seeing her if I want to."

The judge sat back in her chair and listened.

Bryann went on to say... "In the last few minutes of my life, I have learned that my mom had an affair, my father is a bit of a bigot when challenged, my aunt Liv is a stone cold drunk who can't manage to stay sober even through a trial, my parents aren't my biological parents, the woman who birthed me is wicked as hell and I think that guy in the back must be my biological father. I'm assuming that's his wife next to him."

"Go on," the judge said with a wry grin.

"So what is family? It's just a mess of people who love each other. I love my Aunt Liv's drunk ass...oops sorry Judge...and I love it that my mom is not perfect like I always thought she was. I came here in an ambulance from the psycho floor of the hospital-with those two goof balls who know all my family's business now. Honestly, it sounds like everyone in here might need a seventy-two hour hold." She pointed to the back of the courtroom at Kendall's wife. "Especially you...You are nuts for coming here with him. Love must be a powerful thing."

At this point, everyone in the room was smiling. There were some chuckles and even Farah's eyes had dried. She and Greg had clasped hands again. It made Bryann smile, "My parents don't have a perfect marriage. I already knew that. We don't have a perfect family - I thought we did - but I'm glad we don't. It takes the pressure off of me. So since our family isn't perfect and we have cheaters, drunks and bigots, I don't see why we can't at least try to get to know this crazy woman here." She pointed to Riley. "Who has gone Hollywood movie mode crazy to find me."

Bryann saw Greg move forward in his seat. "Sit back Dad. I am your daughter. I love you guys, even more now because you took an imperfect baby. When you found out I was bipolar you could have tossed me back but you didn't. I love you. You are my parents, but I can't ignore this woman who looks just like me...and I'm dying to know the story behind her and the man in the back. I'm happy today because I realize that even though I came here from a mental ward - everybody has a little crazy in them."

The judge smiled and dismissed Bryann. "Thank you sweetheart."

She came down from the stand and gave her parents a hug. The judge requested to see the attorneys in chambers. About ten minutes passed before they returned to the courtroom. Both attorneys whispered to their clients. Riley smiled big. Greg frowned. Farah had a flat look on her face.

The judge banged the gavel. "I have agreed to allow limited visitation for Ms. Briggs at the request of the young

Miss Goodwyn. This visitation will be supervised and it must be attended by at least one of the adoptive parents, preferably both. And I hope you two make it through this. You seem like such a nice family." The judge looked to the back of the courtroom. "Is there anyone else that might feel as if they want to be involved with this beautiful, intelligent, special young lady whom the world is fighting over? Speak now or..."

Kendall and his wife stood up and walked out of the courtroom. Riley yelled, "Kendall!" but he did not respond. She pounded her fist on the desk and the judge shot her a puzzled look.

"Alright then, the details will be worked out and visitation will start no sooner than 14 days and no later than 30 days." The judge hit the gavel one more time and then exited the courtroom.

Greg looked at Farah who was still stunned. "I hope you're happy. So you succeeded in destroying our marriage and our family. Well done. Aunt Janice would be proud."

Farah looked at him, "Greg, just leave me alone. Go wherever it is you go."

-17-

When Farah got back to the house, it was the first time she felt like it was empty. At other times when Greg and Bryann were not home she felt relieved to have a moment to herself. It was usually peaceful, but this day felt empty. Her husband was gone and her daughter was locked away in a psych ward. She could hear her Aunt Janice from the grave, "Ha! I knew you would mess it up."

She walked into the kitchen and pulled a bottle of vodka from beneath the kitchen sink. She had hidden it behind the garbage disposal. She took one small sip from the bottle and put the cap back on top. Farah stood there for a moment more then twisted the top off again and took a big gulp.

"So ten years of sobriety out the window." Greg's voice startled Farah.

She turned around, "I didn't hear you come in. What are you doing here?"

"I live here. I pay the mortgage here," he said. "Let's go get Bryann."

Though Farah was uncertain if Bryann was ready to come home, she decided it was best to go get her daughter. Bryann had made a lot of sense in the courtroom earlier. The notion that she was locked up and the rest of the mentally unhealthy world was out walking freely -wreaking havoc in the lives of others - was indeed a true statement and an injustice for Bryann.

Greg and Farah walked outside and saw that Kane's car was blocking the driveway. "He's at my house!" Greg shouted and started to walk toward Kane. "I've kept my composure long enough with you dude."

"You don't want it to go down like this, Greg. You really don't." Kane started to walk up the driveway toward Greg.

Farah pulled out her phone and sent a text to Callie and Liv "6911" which meant it was a "serious 911". Two grown men about to fight in the front yard was definitely "6911". As opposed to when there was something really crazy going on in their lives it was a "6411". That's what she texted to Liv and Callie when she got the pictures from Riley.

Meanwhile Greg and Kane were blabbing insults at each other across a five-foot space that separated them. Each one encouraged the other to act.

"Set it off," Kane said.

"Go there, " Greg said.

After a few minutes of this, Farah realized that there would be no physical altercation between the two men, but she had already texted everyone. Liv and Adam came running across the neighboring yards that separated their homes. "Greg!" Adam called out. He ran full speed leaving Liv behind.

No sooner than Liv and Adam reached the front yard, Callie pulled up with screeching tires. She jumped out of the car. "Gentleman, this is not a personal courtesy call."

Farah held up her hand to let everyone know it was okay. The two were still exchanging barbs.

"I will slap fire out of you," Kane growled at Greg

"Yeah, and I'll slam your black ass to the ground," Greg gurgled though a gritted teeth.

"There's that 'black' again. You racist bastard!"

"Your ass is black. That's not racist that's a fact so get your black ass off of my property."

By this time Adam had relaxed and Farah, Liv, and Callie were being more entertained than worried. Each of the men took one additional step towards the other but no one was really concerned. Everyone out there understood that there had been way too much talking for a fight to ensue. When people are going to "throw down" it is not usually preceded with colorful dialogue.

Liv looked at Farah, "This was a 6911? I was giving Adam some and you interrupted me for this?"

"I thought it was. It looked like it initially." Farah said as she continued to watch her husband and boyfriend talk about the violent acts they would enact upon if pushed.

"I don't get the '6' anyway. That's silly," Callie said.

"You don't understand?" Farah said.

"No, that's not what I mean." Callie continued. "I mean 411 and 911 speak for themselves. It's silly to add the six in front of it. What's the difference?"

Farah explained as if it were a logical set of rules that must be abided by in life. "The difference between a 911 and a 6911 is you response. 911 means call me now. It's important. 6911 means drop what you are doing and get over here now. It's going down. 411 means I have something to tell you when I see you. 6411 means get over here because I've got some wild stuff to show you."

"Mmm Hmm, " Adam said dismissing Farah. "So how long are we going to let the two of them go on?"

Farah thought for a moment, "Yeah, at this point they are simply background music to our conversation. Callie, go stop them."

"Gentlemen, enough already. Mr. Taylor you are trespassing. I am going to have to ask you to leave." Callie flashed her badge.

Kane looked at Farah, "I'm sorry Babe. I'm really sorry. Please believe I love you."

While Kane flashed softened eyes at Farah waiting for her response, Greg balled up his fist and knocked Kane in the side of the face that was easiest to connect. He knocked him to the ground and stood over him. Kane rolled up from beneath Greg's punch and pulled Greg to the ground. Kane got one punch in. It landed squarely in Greg's left eye before Callie and Adam broke up the fight.

"Sucka punched me," Kane laughed.

"Your lucky I didn't do more than that. Don't you address my wife in my presence Nigga!" Greg screamed. He said nigga like he had grown up in Brooklyn. He said it with a melodic mix of Jay-Z and Chris Rock style. For someone who Farah had never heard utter the word from his lips, he mastered it.

There was a collective "gasp!" that sucked the oxygen out of the air. Kane responded, "See Farah, I told you. Your racist husband knows the word. He uses it when he can."

"This has nothing to do with you being black. You idiot! You screw my wife. You come to my house and tell my wife you love her right in front of my face. In the words of my best friend over there..." Greg pointed to Adam. "...that's some nigga shit!"

"It sure is," Adam agreed.

"I mean, true." Liv concurred.

Even Farah shrugged in agreement.

Callie cuffed Kane's hands behind his back. "You want to go home or you want to go to jail?" she asked him.

"Let go of me," Kane wiggled in the handcuffs. "Farah, please listen to me."

"I don't want to hear anything you have to say. Get off of my property. Stay away from my family and do not ever contact me again." She turned and walked into the house.

"But Farah..." Kane yelled again.

Greg followed Farah into the house. Liv and Adam walked behind Greg. A few minutes later Callie came through the front door. "He's gone."

Farah nestled next to Greg on the sofa. "Thank you honey."

He jerked his shoulder from under her head. "Don't thank me. I was defending my home and my manhood, not you. That's the guy you love. You told me so. So, now that you've learned who he really is you don't love him anymore?"

"I was misled," Farah said.

"And now I'm supposed to forget it ever happened and we just move along."

Adam interjected, "Maybe you guys should talk about this later...ummm, when we aren't all sitting here."

"No, it's all family. You guys have been just as much apart of this an anyone." He pointed to Callie and Liv.

"No they have not," Farah said. "Don't put them in this."

"You put them in this!"

Callie stood up, "Oh dear God, I'll call you later. I'm going back to my phone sex." She walked out.

Adam stood to his feet and motioned for liv to follow. She shook her head and remained seated with her legs crossed and her arms folded. Adam barked, "Olive Jones."

"What?" Liv said, "So if you growl that's going to make me get up. I said no."

"Woman, are you crazy. Let's go home." Adam reached for her arm and she snatched away.

"I'm not leaving them. Look..." She turned to Greg and Farah, "you guys need to decide whether to stay together or call it quits. Greg, don't act like there were no problems between you two until Kane came along. We know that's not true."

"Olive!" Adam shouted. "Mind your business."

"This is your best friend, isn't it? Then why aren't you trying to help. Men are so... just...."

"Not meddlesome? Mind their own business?" Adam finished for her.

"No! So simple. Just La Di Da about everything. Our best friends are in trouble and we are here to help."

Greg and Farah looked at each other and smiled. Farah whispered, "We made them fight."

They both giggled softly while they listened to Adam and Liv go on and on about the differences between men and women. Adam asserted that women should stay out of everyone's business. Liv argued that men should be more engaged in what's happening with their friends and family.

"There's more to life than making money," Liv said.

"Clearly, that would be YOUR life..."

Adam's retort got to Liv, "OH, that's it. I'm getting a job. You forgot I am a Georgetown graduate? Top of my law school class."

"Who hasn't practiced law in eleven years. Don't be ridiculous." Adam sat back down on the love seat next to Liv, who winked at Farah. Whenever Liv spoke of getting a job she snatched the rug from under Adam's feet. She knew he loved having a stay-at-home wife who was pampered.

"Well played," Greg laughed.

The four sat together and talked about how crazy the last few months had been with Riley, Kane, and the biological father showing up. They recapped Bryann's testimony on the witness stand and Liv laughed at the way her dear niece characterized her as a drunk. No one else laughed.

"How is Bryann?" Adam asked.

"We were on our way to get her when Kane showed up." Farah looked at Greg.

He flopped back on the sofa. "Yeah, that sure stopped the show."

"Not really," Liv said, "It was more painful to listen to all that rhetoric."

They all laughed.

"I'm going to miss you Dr. Goodwyn." Greg kissed Farah on the cheek.

Farah had a puzzled look across her face, "Miss me?"

He leaned in and rested his elbows on his thighs. Dropped his head and lifted it again. He looked at his best friends in the world, of whom he included Farah. "I want a divorce."

Liv stood up, "We'll let you guys talk."

"Oh now you want to let them talk." Adam shook his head. He gave Greg a grip and kissed Farah on the cheek. "We are here for both of you. Whichever way you choose. We know you'll do what's best for all of you...including Bryann."

"Come on guilt trip," Liv motioned for Adam as she walked to the door. "Geez...could you be any more obvious."

Greg and Farah laughed as they watched their best friends exit. "Those two were made for each other," Greg said.

"Yup," Farah agreed.

"But were we?" Greg asked. He had a serious look in his eyes. He really wanted to know the answer from Farah.

She thought about just playing it out as her Aunt Janice had written for her so long ago. The big house, the perfect husband, the great neighbors in an excellent neighborhood. Instead, she said, "No. I don't think we were. I adore you but..."

"But there is no passion between us," Greg finished. "We're parenting partners. Roommates."

"You want to go to counseling?" Farah asked.

"Not really."

"You're done?" Farah asked.

"I think I am," Greg said. He looked at her. "Do you love him?"

Tears welled in Farah's eyes. She was angry with Kane and she felt foolish. As a psychiatrist she should have seen the behavior. Even Quiana warned her about him. Farah was sick to her stomach with every thought of the time they made love or shared a laugh together. She was embarrassed. She answered Greg's question, "No. Absolutely not."

"Did you?"

"I thought I did, but it all turned out to be a game," Farah mumbled.

"But if it weren't a game you would be in love with him still."

"Probably," Farah said.

He nodded. He stood up and pulled her close to him. Greg squeeze Farah with all the love he had over the almost twenty years of marriage. "Let's go get our daughter."

Farah smiled and they walked hand in hand out the door.

-18-

It was sure to be an interesting day. Farah had planned a birthday luncheon with Bryann, Callie, Liv, and Riley Briggs. Since the day Farah brought Bryann back to the United States she dreaded the moment when her daughter would find out she was adopted. That moment came. It was more awful than Farah could have imagined, but over the months she had gotten used to the notion that Riley Briggs would be apart of their lives.

Bryann came downstairs in a dress that could have been airbrushed on. "Excuse." Farah said. "What do you have on your body?"

Bryann looked down. "A dress. It's the dress Riley sent me."

Farah swallowed hard. "And you want to wear it to lunch to show your appreciation?"

"Yes. That's the right thing to do, right?" Bryann winced.

Farah could see that Bryann was nervous. "Yes, it is. You like it?"

"Mom, look at it. No! I look like a Vegas escort."

"Bryann!" Farah laughed. She was relieved that Riley had posed no threat to her relationship with Bryann. Bryann was Farah's daughter through and through. She was more like Farah than anyone else in the world. They shared the same taste in clothes, movies, and food. Farah was still Bryann's hero and she was glad.

Just then, Liv and Callie rang the doorbell before walking into the house. "Hey! It's girls day!" Callie squealed. Farah appreciated her efforts.

"I'm starving," Liv said. "You ready for lunch Birthday girl?"

"Auntie Liv, I know we are all dreading this. Let's not pretend that we don't. I'll be fifteen years old tomorrow, not five."

Farah snapped her fingers. "Oh what time is your dad picking you up tomorrow? He asked me to gather some things for him."

Callie grimaced, "How is Greg? I miss him."

"He's good. He bought the serious bachelor pad and a new sports car. He's ready to be on the market." Farah laughed. She was happy for Greg. They were both happier.

"Wow! How does he handle all that and the mortgage too?" Callie asked.

Liv said, "Girl, Greg makes enough money to pay Farah's mortgage, my mortgage and your phone bill with all those 900 calls."

They all laughed, including Bryann.

Callie hugged Bryann. "Hey! What are you laughing at?"

The three women and one newly crowned young woman locked arms. "Well, let's go have our family luncheon," Farah said with excitement.

Liv chuckled. "Yes, we should be called the 'sisterhood of six degrees' since we are all jumbled together through all these different connections."

Bryann thought for a moment. "You know, you're right Auntie Liv. Think about how crazy this is." Bryann went on to explain. "Auntie Callie was adopted by the family that lived next door to Mom who was being raised by Aunt Janice. She met Dad whose childhood best friend married you. Mom and Dad got married and adopted me. Now Riley comes back on the scene. We are all connected in a crazy way."

Callie pondered it. "Yeah, if our lives had been perfect, we never would have met each other. If I had not been a foster child, I would have never ended up living next door to Farah."

Farah interjected, "And if my mother had not died, I wouldn't have even been living with Aunt Janice to meet you. And growing up with Aunt Janice forced me into dating someone like Greg."

"Who's best friend is my incredible husband," Liv added.

Callie laughed. "We really are the sista'hood of six degrees. And You know I am as much a sista as you guys are. Remember, I was raised by a Black woman."

Bryann interjected, "Oh nobody forgets that, Aunt Callie. Believe me!" Bryann laughed and kissed Callie on the cheek. "But that's a lame name for you guys. You need a better name than that."

Farah thought for a moment and a coy grin spread across her face. "How about..."

To be continued…

"GATHERING MOSS" (December 2014)

Read an excerpt from the rest of the story...

Farah was unsure how she would ever make it through the afternoon luncheon. She felt her stomach drop when she arrived at the restaurant and saw her daughter's birthmother standing out front. Riley always managed to pull off a look that was both trashy, yet amazingly graceful all at once. In a dress that appeared to be airbrushed onto her perfectly fit body, she showcased a plunging neckline and a hemline that cupped her buttocks.

"Hey Ladies!" Riley shouted.

"Hi Riley," Farah said while inhaling a deep cleansing breath.

Of course, Liv extended a welcoming hug to Riley. She was always the peacemaker and Farah knew that if she was going to be able to pull off this luncheon she would have to lean on Liv's grace.

Callie, on the other hand, simply nodded in Riley's direction. She had yet to get over all of Riley's antics from a few months ago. Callie had conducted a full investigation into Riley's sordid past. There was nothing criminal but certainly a long list of sketchy, questionable social behavior. Riley's behavior with men made escorts and call girls wince.

"Happy Birthday! How's my girl?" Riley asked Bryann. "Oh I see you are wearing the dress I bought you. Do you like it?"

Bryann looked at Farah. "Ummm, yeah. It's not something I would usually wear but I'm open to it."

"Good!" Riley said and smoothed her hands down her hips and thighs. "You have the same amazing body I have so we gotta teach you how to flaunt it."

"Oh I am not so sure that is necessary at fifteen," Farah interjected.

"Please! Fifteen in some cultures is considered a women who can marry and bear children." Riley said with a smile to Bryann.

Farah saw Byrann's discomfort building. She did not want her daughter to be tense or upset for her birthday, or any other day for that matter. So Farah took another deep breath and smiled, "I suppose you are right, but my fifteen year old daughter will not be one of them."

"OUR daughter," Riley corrected.

With that comment, Callie abruptly called out to the good-looking older gentleman standing behind the podium. "Excuse me handsome. We are the Goodwyn party of five."

The gentleman blushed and instructed the girls to follow him to a private room just off of the patio. It was a beautiful cozy room that could probably accommodate ten people, but for the day it was just the five of them. When Bryann entered the room she gasped.

"Mom! I love it." She leaned into Farah and gave her a tight hug. Farah felt the love of Bryann penetrate her bones. Bryann was the first thing in Farah's life that ever mattered to her. So making her happy each and every day was a priority. "Oh my goodness! Purple and pink butterflies everywhere. Thank you Mommy!"

"You're very welcome baby! Let's all sit down."

The waiter moved in and out of the room quickly. He returned with five champagne flutes. Bryann's eyes lit up like a diamonds before the waiter said, "Birthday girl…your sparkling cider." He bowed as if she were a princess.

"Mom!"

"Yes?" Farah looked at her.

"Oh come on Farah. It's her birthday. If she lived in Europe she could drink a year ago." Riley grabbed a glass from the waiter and placed it in front of Bryann who grinned.

Farah cleared her throat and the waiter retrieved the glass from in front of Bryann and placed it in front of Liv who quickly swallowed it before grabbing another. "Okay, here we go," Liv said under her breath.

Callie remained quiet but her eyes shot flaming arrows across the table at Riley. Farah began to wonder if this luncheon was a good idea. If these ladies could not make it though a two-hour lunch together there was no way they could spend the next twelve months planning Bryann's sweet sixteen.

After everyone had full glasses Farah proposed a toast. "Happy Birthday to my beautiful baby girl…" she looked over at Riley. "…The sweet daughter that we all share. Baby, we are all here together as the women who love you. You can come to us for anything."

Get reader's guides, discussion maps, and more on

www.KamrynAdams.com

Connect with Kamryn Adams on Social media
Facebook.com/kamrynadams
Twitter.com/kamrynadams
Instragram.com/kamrynadams
Pintrest.com/kamrynpins
Kamrynadams.blogspot.com

Email: Kamryn@KamrynAdams.com